aHunter4Ever

By

Cynthia A Clement

Cover designed by RomCon® www.romcon.com

Cover Image: The Killion Group, Inc.

www.thekilliongroupinc.com

Dedication

To Susan.

Her course, The Pirate Principles, taught me to value my treasure and silence my parrot.

Chapter 1

She lured him like a siren.

Eighteen years a warrior and he was as weak as the first day he had held a weapon. If he had any defense against her magnetism, he would have turned the car around and went back to his unit. It was dangerous. His team was too far away to come to his rescue if this was a trap. Yet, he continued onward.

He could not deny the attraction.

He was powerless to resist.

He was a Hunter. An elite warrior from another planet who was stranded on Earth along with the other members of his unit. He was part of a brotherhood of warriors who had made it their mission to help those who needed justice. They kept a low profile and avoided law enforcement officers. He was breaking the first rule of survival by returning alone to a house where so many FBI agents were gathered.

He needed to finish his mission.

The guard at the entrance to the Beverly Hills mansion waved him up to the house. A shiver of awareness skittered across the back of Partlan's neck as he drove through the ornate metal gates. He was drawn here by a force that was greater than his training. In the past, implants and chemical modifications had prevented Hunters from forming a pair bond and mating. All that had changed since they had crashed on Earth.

He told himself that the child he had helped rescue deserved to be returned to his parents by him. He had been the leader of the team that had been hired to find the children. That was not the complete truth. He came back to this house because he had to see her one more time. He had to be certain that the connection he felt between them was real.

Beside him, Gates Walters, was fidgeting with his seatbelt. Gates was the son of Nikki Nevins and Steve Walters, A-list actors and Hollywood royalty. Gates was of slight build and short for a boy of eight, but given that both his parents were tall, he would probably grow. The boy had been quiet for most of the journey from Caliente. That was where they had found Gates and several other children. They were being held in a building used by a group of child traffickers.

Partlan glanced down at him, noting that the hazel eyes turned up at him were huge with sadness.

"What will happen to Tarrin?"

Tarrin and Gates had been raised together by Tarrin's mother Selena. She was Gates's nanny, but the busy schedule of actors had meant that Gates spent most of his time with Selena and Tarrin. The two boys had been kidnapped together. It had been Tarrin's mother, Selena, who had contacted them for help. Selena had since reconciled with her mate Catal, who was also a Hunter and Tarrin's father. That made the boy a Hunter. He was the first child ever born to their breed and needed training in their ways.

"He is with his brothers now." Partlan slowed the vehicle as he approached the front door. "Tarrin must learn the ways of a warrior."

"I wish I could stay with him."

"Your place is with your parents."

"They don't want me." Gates's voice was matter of fact. "Tarrin and Selena were my family."

"Then, you will see them again." Partlan shifted the car into park. "Family can never be parted."

Gates's eyes were intense as they surveyed Partlan's face. "Promise?"

"Those we love are with us, even in death." Partlan placed a hand over his heart. "They live with us always."

"Did your parents love you?"

"I did not have a mother or father." Partlan noted the FBI agent guarding the door. "Hunters are bred from machines."

"If you don't have a family, then how do you know that they are with you?"

"All Hunters are brothers. We are family, and when one is killed in battle, we still feel their presence with us."

"Tarrin isn't going to die, is he?"

"He has his father to protect him."

"I wish my father was like that." Gates's voice was low. "He's too busy for me."

Partlan had struggled these past months on Earth to understand humans. His whole life had been dedicated to righting wrongs so that others could live without worries. Humans had freedoms that had been denied him, and they threw them away without thought. There was no reason or logic to their behavior.

He reached into the upper pocket of his combat vest and pulled out a card and pen. He circled a website and then added a telephone number before handing it to Gates. "If you ever need to contact Tarrin, or any Hunter, use this."

Gates looked down at the card. "Is this where Tarrin is?"

"An email or phone call will connect you with Tarrin or his father, Catal." Partlan watched Gates put the card into his pants pocket. "I will stay with you until you are safe with your family."

Gates nodded. "The bad men won't get me again. I'll be smarter next time."

A child should not have to live in fear, but there was no way for Partlan to undo what had happened to Gates. He had been kidnapped, held captive, and sold to a child trafficking group. If his team had not found the boys in time, they would have been lost forever. The crimes that were done on this planet were unforgivable.

"You must always be on guard." Partlan kept his voice calm. "If you fear, contact us. We will protect you."

"Can you teach me to be as strong and brave as you?" Gates's voice held a note of determination.

"You must let go of your fear or it will imprison you and keep you weak. As you grow older, this will be easier. Already you are braver than most boys your age." Partlan unlatched his seatbelt and opened the car door. The FBI agent was motioning for them to enter the house. "We must go."

Gates scooted across the front seat and jumped down beside Partlan. He took his hand and together they walked to the door. The agent put his hand on Partlan's chest to stop him from going inside. Gates gripped him tighter.

"Only the boy." The agent's voice was filled with menace. "You're to come with me."

"No." Gates's voice was firm. "I need Partlan. He stays with me."

The agent hesitated a second and then nodded. "No funny stuff."

They walked into the large dark marble floored foyer. A massive crystal chandelier hung in the center of the ceiling and the walls were covered in a soft-green silk material. They were led to the room where Partlan had first met Steve Walters and his wife Nikki

Nevins. The door was opened by Agent Bakker who followed them into the room and stood guard at the door.

When they entered, Gates's parents were sitting on a dark brown sectional and Agent Kelly was standing beside them. She looked at him directly and tilted her head. Partlan's chest tightened. His heart soared at seeing her.

Her blonde hair was tied back in a tight bun at the back of her head and her dark blue eyes flashed anger. She was wearing a loose pant suit that hid her body. Nikki Nevins was also blonde and blue-eyed, with a curvaceous figure accentuated by a tight fitting top and pants, but she did not affect him. It was more than a physical attraction that had drawn him back to this place. Seeing Agent Kelly again only confirmed what he had already suspected.

They were connected.

"Gates!" Nikki was the first to move. She ran to her son, knelt, and wrapped her arms around him. "You're safe."

Nikki picked Gates up and went to Steve. Steve rubbed the boy's head and then hugged him. They sat, with Gates between them, on the couch. Nikki looked up at Partlan and smiled.

"Thank you." Tears ran down her cheeks. "After what Agent Kelly told us about the boys being sold, I didn't think we would ever see our son again."

"Hunters do not fail." Partlan spread his legs and crossed his arms over his chest. "We reached the boys before any harm could be done."

"How can you say that?" Agent Kelly's voice was low with reproach. "From what I understand, you left a number of bodies in your wake. I'm happy the boys were returned, but did they have to experience so much killing?"

"Would you rather we had left them in the hands of the traffickers?" Partlan's tone was dry. "We did what was necessary. The men who held the boys refused to give them up. They shot first."

"That does not excuse the mess you left behind." Agent Kelly's voice was defensive. "The law does not tolerate vigilantism."

"The FBI have a point." Steve Walter shifted away from Gates on the couch. "My son shouldn't have been exposed to violence. Once you knew where the men were located, you should have contacted the police and let them take care of the situation."

"You asked us to return your son. You made it clear you did not care how that was done, or who was hurt." Partlan did not hide his contempt for Steve. The man was a coward who had been negligent and partly to blame for the children being kidnapped in the first place.

Steve's eyes narrowed. Before he could speak, his wife, Nikki put a hand on her husband's arm. "Partlan's right. We did give him permission to use any means to get Gates back home. I don't care if those men are dead."

"Gates did not see anything." Partlan's voice was firm. "We are not new at rescue missions. We kept the children protected."

"I hope so." Nikki turned to Gates. "Were you hurt?"

Gates shook his head. "Partlan and Tarrin's father kept us safe."

"Tarrin's father?" Agent Kelly's eyes widened. "I thought no one knew who he was? Was he involved in the kidnapping?"

"Catal is Tarrin's father."

"So Selena lied to us." Agent Kelly's lips thinned. "Where are they now?"

"They are safe."

"They need to answer questions. It's suspicious that Catal should suddenly admit to being the boy's father."

"He did not know." Partlan's voice was matter of fact.

He was not going to elaborate further. Selena had not realized she was pregnant when she had run away from Catal. She had remained in hiding for eight years and it was only the kidnapping of Tarrin that had forced her to contact Catal for help. That was when Selena had learned that Catal had never betrayed her. It was a matter between Catal and his mate Selena, to explain the situation if they wished it known.

"That's pretty convenient." Agent Kelly's gaze never left Partlan. "Unfortunately, that won't hold up in a court of law. I need to be certain he wasn't in on the kidnapping with Selena."

"Catal saved us." Gates's voice rose. "Leave him alone."

"It's understandable that you're thankful to your rescuers." Agent Kelly's voice was sympathetic. "The law sees things differently."

"I know Catal wasn't the man who kidnapped us." Gates crossed his arms. "Why don't you find those men and yell at them."

Partlan caught Gate's eye and nodded his approval. The boy was getting stronger. The kidnapping might have been traumatic, but Gates was learning to let go of fear.

"We have the Gordon brothers in custody." Agent Kelly turned away from Gates. "We need to speak with your men."

Partlan shook his head. "They have returned to our unit."

"Tell me where they are." Agent Kelly pulled a pad from her pocket. "We need to question them."

"I cannot do that." Partlan clenched his jaw. "No Hunter would betray his brothers."

"This is serious." Agent Kelly took a step toward him. "You could be facing jail time for the killings. If you refuse to help us, we could arrest you and put you in prison for obstruction of justice."

"A Hunter is never free." Partlan's voice was devoid of emotion. "I have survived torture, pain, injury, and loss, but never have I broken my vow. There is nothing you can do to me that will change that."

Surprise and disbelief raced across Agent Kelly's face, but Partlan remained firm in his resolve. No matter what the attraction between them, he would not betray his brothers. They depended on him to keep them safe. If he were in danger, they would do the same thing.

"You leave me no choice but to arrest you."

"You can try."

The tension in the room was a living, breathing entity.

Nikki Nevins cleared her throat. "There must be another way to deal with this. These men were hired by us to find Gates. They weren't involved in the kidnapping."

"We don't know that." Agent Kelly turned to Nikki. "The reports I have from the Caliente police are describing a massacre. We can't have vigilantes running around handing out their own brand of justice."

"Those men took us and were mean." Gates jutted his chin out.

"My hands are tied." Agent Kelly sighed. "My job is to make sure that the law is obeyed."

"It's stupid." Gates threw himself back on the couch. "Partlan is a hero."

"Anyone can take a gun and kill people. That doesn't make them a hero." Agent Kelly's voice was reasonable.

"I think you might make an exception here. It sounds as if they had to kill those men in self defense." Nikki's tone was conciliatory. "I asked them to help and they only stepped in once your ransom drop failed."

Agent Kelly lifted her chin. "We didn't fail. We did everything by the book."

"It did not work." Partlan spoke without emotion.

Agent Kelly was not going to let him go without a fight. Part of him wanted to stay with her and answer her questions, but it would be useless. There was a connection between them, but she was not ready. She had a wall built around her that would not come down easily. He sensed that she did not want him or any person in her life.

"That's because you interfered." Agent Kelly crossed her arms over her chest. "You could have come to us with your suspicions. Instead, you took the law into your own hands."

"We did what you could not."

"You broke the law." A muscle in Agent Kelly's jaw tightened. "You leave me no choice. I need to take you in for questioning."

"The law of this world does not hold us. We are Hunters and live by the Sacred Code of our forefathers."

"So this code allows you to kill people willy-nilly?"

"We kill those who have no honor." Partlan rolled the tension from his shoulders. This was an argument that had no purpose. Humans did not understand that there was only one punishment for breaking the first law of the Sacred Code and that was death. "Those who hurt women or children have broken the code."

"You obstructed justice." Agent Kelly shook her head and pulled a set of handcuffs from her under her jacket. "You're under arrest."

Partlan raised an eyebrow. "Is that what you really want to do?"

"Just as you have your code to live by, I have a duty to protect people from those who break the law."

"I ensured that your laws were followed."

"We will have to investigate further to be certain." Agent Kelly took a step toward him. "Until then, you need to come with me."

Partlan shook his head and turned to the door. "Your rules make no sense."

Agent Bakker moved away from the door with his gun drawn. "Stop, or I will shoot you."

Partlan looked over his shoulder. Agent Kelly's one hand was raised and she was motioning for him to stop. Her eyes were narrowed, her lips pursed, and her other hand was reaching inside of her jacket. Her intent was clear. She did not want him to leave the room. Still, he could not let himself be captured. On his home planet, he would have obeyed a woman, but since landing on Earth, he knew they did not always rule with logic.

She was a woman he was connected to.

He would not fight her.

"I will not be held by your laws." Partlan turned to face her. "I will not hurt a woman."

"Good." Agent Kelly threw the cuffs at him. They landed with a soft thud on the area rug where Partlan was standing. "Put these on."

"No." Partlan walked backwards to the door. "I will leave you with information where you can contact me with your questions."

"Stop." Agent Kelly and Agent Bakker shouted together.

"Don't think I won't shoot you." Agent Bakker had moved close to him.

Partlan reached into his jacket for a card.

Agent Bakker took a step closer and pulled the trigger of his weapon.

The loud retort of a gun ripped through the air.

Pain shot through Partlan's shoulder. He took a step back and looked down at the blood seeping through his upper left chest. It left a trail down the front of his torn shirt and his skin was blackened around a small hole where the bullet had entered. He looked up at Agent Kelly and saw the dismay on her face. He sent her a wave of forgiveness. He could not blame her. Her laws might be wrong, but it was her duty to follow them. Just as it was his duty to leave. He took an unsteady step backwards.

"I'll shoot again." Agent Bakker's voice was cold.

Before Partlan could take another step, the door opened and two FBI agents rushed in. They grabbed him. He fought them off and turned away just as another agent pushed him to the ground. A searing pain ripped through his shoulder and for a second he thought he'd been shot again. He recognized the agent who'd tackled him and was pressing his hand against his wound. It was Agent Smythe.

Partlan struggled to get up, but another two other agents jumped on him. He was losing blood and a wave of weakness washed over him. He was finding it harder to breath and he did not think he would be able to prevent his imprisonment. He closed his eyes and sent out a mind connection to Ardal, his leader, to let him know of his capture. Before he could finish his report, a jolt of massive energy pulsed through him.

Every muscle in his body went rigid.

Immense pain followed.

The last thing he heard was Agent Kelly's voice. There was a note of panic in her tone. "Call an ambulance."

Chapter 2

The gunshot reverberated around the room.

Blood oozed from Partlan's chest and that's when the reality of the situation hit her. Agent Grace Kelly shuddered as a wave of revulsion skittered through her body. Her stomach churned with nausea. She'd been involved in shoot outs with criminals before, but never had she'd experienced this gut wrenching panic. It was primal in its intensity. It was as if she'd been shot herself, which was ridiculous.

She watched Smythe subdue the prisoner, pushing his hand against the wound in Partlan's chest. The man was a sadist. Then Smythe brought out his stun gun and held it against Partlan's side and shocked him until his body jerked in response. The words froze in her throat as she tried to scream at Smythe to stop. She shook with reaction.

Partlan looked up at her.

There was acceptance in his eyes.

"Call an ambulance." It was her voice, but the words sounded as if they'd come from someone else.

She rushed to Partlan and pushed Smythe off his limp body. "He's not going anywhere."

"Best to play it safe with this one." Smythe stood and kicked Partlan in the side.

"Is that necessary?" Nikki Nevins voice rose in outrage. "The man brought our son back to us and this is the best you can do?"

"He's a criminal." Agent Smythe straightened his dark suit coat. "You should thank us for making the world a safer place."

"He made it safer, not you." Nikki turned to her sobbing son and pulled him into her arms. "The only thing the FBI has done is lose our money and let our son's kidnappers get away. Now you've exposed Gates to horrific violence. I'm sorry we ever called you in for help."

"Your son is alive." Smythe spoke without emotion. "Do you know how rare that is in a kidnapping?"

"Enough."

Grace used her most authoritative tone. The situation was deteriorating faster than she could control. An agent in charge never allowed that. She straightened her shoulders and let her training take over.

"Smythe, you can leave. Contact the field office and apprise them of the new developments."

For a second she thought he was going to disobey a direct order. He looked at her, his brown eyes narrowed and then he shrugged. He left the room with a slam of the door. Bakker had holstered his weapon and was on the floor beside Partlan. He pulled a pistol out of Partlan's waistband and put it into a clear evidence bag.

"I thought he was reaching for his gun."

"Well it wasn't in his upper pocket." Grace subdued a shiver that raced across her body. "What was he trying to get?"

Bakker reached into the pocket of Partlan's green military style vest and pulled out a piece of paper. "It's a business card."

He handed Grace the card. She looked down at the light beige stock and noted the print. There was only one line. aHunter4Hire.com. Nothing else. This must have been how Selena had contacted them.

"Should I cuff him?" Bakker picked up the cuffs she had thrown at Partlan. They were on the rug beside him.

"He's not going anywhere."

Bakker nodded and continued to search Partlan's pockets. Grace forced her eyes away. Looking at Partlan was causing her insides to twist. It wasn't the sight of blood, or an unconscious prisoner that upset her. It was the lifelessness of his body. He affected her like no other man had ever done before. It was as if his misery, was hers.

She turned back to the Walters family. Steve was sitting on the couch with his arms crossed and a scowl on his face. Nikki was holding her son close and running a comforting hand over his head. Anger and disbelief flashed from Nikki's eyes. Grace cleared her throat. No matter how she felt, she was still a Federal Agent and responsible for the welfare of these people.

"I'm sorry for the disturbance."

"You call shooting a man in my living room a disturbance?" Steve Walters' lip curled into a sneer. "I'll be billing the FBI for damages."

"That's understandable Mr. Walters. As soon as the ambulance arrives, we'll be out of here." Grace gestured toward Partlan. "He gave us no choice."

"He didn't threaten you." Nikki's voice sounded brittle. "You could have let him go."

"That wasn't possible. Agent Bakker shot because he thought Partlan was going for a weapon."

Grace whispered the words as she turned back to her prisoner. He was still motionless on the floral area rug where he'd fallen. His breathing was ragged and there were bubbles coming from his wound. She knelt beside him and pressed her hand against his wound to slow the blood and air loss. Already his shirt was bright red and there were splatters of blood on the rug. He looked lifeless, but she could feel the steady beat of his heart beneath her hand.

She willed him to hold on. He might be a criminal, but he didn't deserve to die. The siren of an approaching ambulance eased some of the tension that was building within her. She had too many questions. She needed him alive. None of his answers would explain the connection she felt with him, though.

He was a stranger she'd only met a couple of days ago.

She felt as if he were the only person she had ever known.

The paramedics rushed into the room. They rolled him over to check for an exit wound, but there was none. The next few minutes were taken up with applying a clear bandage over the wound and then trying to lift Partlan onto the stretcher. It took four of them and when he was situated on it, they rolled him out of the room. Grace kept pace with them. She wasn't about to let anyone else have access to Partlan, or give him a chance to escape.

"Tell Smythe to finish here." Grace issued her orders to Bakker as she climbed into the back of the ambulance with the paramedics. "You head back to the office. You'll need to hand in your weapon and make a report. As soon as I know the prisoner's condition, I'll debrief you."

Bakker nodded and turned back to the house just as the rear door of the ambulance shut the rest of the world out. The vehicle drove away with siren and lights on. The paramedic in the rear with her, grabbed one of Partlan's arms and inserted an IV. He hooked up a bag of saline and then cut off Partlan's shirt and camo vest so he could hook up electrodes to his chest.

For the first time, she was able to see the full extent of the damage done to Partlan. The 9mm bullet had ripped a smooth hole through his chest. The area was surrounded by a ring of abrasion and gunshot residue. She swallowed back the bile that rose in her throat. She'd seen gun wounds before, but they'd never affected her like this one.

Partlan was a confessed vigilante with no respect for the law, so why did she care? For a brief second, she wondered if she'd done the right thing trying to arrest him. She could have let him walk away. He'd brought down a huge child trafficking ring and captured two kidnappers. In most people's eyes, he was a hero.

A groan brought her attention back to her prisoner. His eyelids fluttered and he looked straight at her. Her breath caught in her throat at the intense compassion and acceptance she saw deep in his dark eyes.

"Do not blame yourself." His words were a hoarse whisper before his lids closed and his head rolled to the side.

Alarms screeched.

The paramedic jumped up and started CPR. "We're losing him. Can you do this while I set up the defibrillator?"

There was no time for thought, only action. Grace took over the compressions. She counted them out in her head, one, two, three, until she lost all sense of time as her first aid training kicked in. The paramedic worked beside her and she heard the whining sound of the machine charging up. "Clear." His command reverberated through the ambulance.

Grace removed her hands.

The paddles were placed on his chest.

It took three jolts before the steady rhythm of a heartbeat sounded on the monitor. The paramedic stepped back and wiped his forehead with the sleeve of his uniform just as the ambulance pulled into the hospital. Grace was pushed aside as the stretcher was unloaded and Partlan was rushed into the emergency. She sagged against the back of the ambulance and fought for breath.

It was crazy, but when Partlan had crashed, she'd thought she was dying. Her hands were shaking. She shoved them into the pockets of her suit coat. She exhaled and straightened her shoulders. She had struggled long and hard to gain the respect of her peers and supervisors. She wasn't going to lose it now. She had a job to do. It didn't matter how she was affected by her prisoner. She went through the hospital doors and pulled out her credentials. She was taking control of herself and the prisoner.

Once the hospital had been informed that their patient was a prisoner, she contacted the field office and arranged to have a guard for him. The emergency room doctor had already advised her that Partlan had gone straight to surgery and it would be several hours before she'd hear anything about his condition. She fought the urge to stay. She was still the agent in charge. She needed to get to the Walters' house to debrief her agents and the family before this got out of control.

When she reached the Beverly Hills mansion, there were a number of agents loading computers and equipment into agency vans. She went in and saw that most of their control room was cleared out. Smythe was standing in the doorway and barking out orders. She braced herself for a confrontation.

"Is he going to live?" Smythe's tone was derogatory. "Or is the world a safer place?"

Grace took a deep breath and tamped down her anger. She knew Smythe thought he was doing his job, but the force he'd used had been excessive. It wouldn't matter to his career, though. He could claim that he had perceived a threat and taken the necessary action. The fact that Partlan had disarmed her the first time she had met him, would add credence to his claim.

"He crashed on the way to the hospital. They stabilized him and he's in surgery now. We need to talk."

"What's the problem?"

"You didn't have to shock him. He was already on the ground." Grace kept her tone neutral. "The kick was unprofessional."

"He's stronger than three men put together. I wasn't taking any chances." Smythe crossed his arms over his chest. "It was my call. I'm sure the Chief won't have a problem with it."

"I have no choice but to put this in my report."

"I wouldn't expect less of you Kelly." Smythe turned back to the control room. "The family's waiting in the living room. Bakker debriefed them before he left."

She squared her shoulders and went to meet with the Walters. Nikki Nevins had already made her position about arresting Partlan very clear. What Grace needed to do was calm the family down and assure them that the FBI was working in the best interest of the public's safety.

The family were seated on the couch when she entered the living room. The rug Partlan had fallen on, and stained with his blood, had been removed. Everything else was the same. She took a deep breath and forced a smile to her face.

"Is he going to be okay?" Gates small voice trembled.

"He's in surgery now, but he should pull through." Grace kept her tone optimistic. She wouldn't allow herself to think of what the consequences might be if he died.

"What do you want Agent Kelly?" Nikki's voice was devoid of emotion.

"We are clearing our equipment out of your house and I wanted to be certain that you will be able to handle things once we're gone."

"My son has been returned alive." Nikki pursed her lips. "The way his rescuer was handled is another matter."

"We will be investigating everything that Partlan did to get your son back." Grace walked closer to the family. "We know that people were killed in the execution of Gates's rescue. I need to be certain that Partlan wasn't involved in anything criminal."

Steve Walters leaned forward. "When can we have our house back?"

"Within the hour." Grace cleared her throat. "Is there anything else we can do for you?"

"I think you've done more than enough." Nikki turned away from Grace.

"I wanted to tell you how happy I am that Gates was returned to you alive." Grace looked down for a second before facing the family again. "It's not often that we have such a happy outcome."

"After seeing how you work, I can understand that." Nikki's voice was a sharp reprimand.

Grace nodded and left the room. There was nothing else she could say. They were unhappy about the shooting and she couldn't blame them. Hopefully they would focus on how lucky they were to have Gates returned alive. Usually the outcome of a kidnapping ended in death. They had their son back and they would soon get over the inconvenience of having their house overrun by Federal Agents. Maybe one day they'd even forget that a man had been shot in their living room.

Grace would remember it the rest of her life.

She waited until everything had been cleared out of the house and her agents had returned to the office before going back to the hospital. It was her responsibility to make certain the prisoner survived. This one was personal. Deep within her was a need to know if he lived. She sensed he still did, but she needed the doctors to tell her he was alive.

She sat in one of the faux suede chairs in the surgery waiting room. She'd informed the nurses that she would need to speak with the surgeon when he was finished. Now all she could do was wait. She leaned back and shut her eyes. The shooting kept replaying in her mind. It was useless to try and rest. She pulled out her phone and started to check emails.

It was several hours later before she heard anything about Partlan's condition.

The surgeon walked into the waiting room still in surgical scrubs. Grace put away her cell phone and went over to him.

"I'm Special Agent Kelly." She held her hand out and shook his hand. "How's my prisoner?"

"He'll survive." The surgeon crossed his arms over his chest. "I would have thought the bullet would have been enough to stop him. Shocking him was a bit excessive."

"I've talked to the agent responsible."

"You can tell him from me that he probably caused your prisoner's heart to stop. Next time he needs to have a bit more care before using that thing on an already wounded man."

She shifted on her feet. "He was in the ambulance before his heart stopped."

"That jolt of electricity didn't help. He was already losing blood from the bullet wound and his lungs were compromised. It's lucky he's in perfect physical condition."

"How long before I can see him?"

Grace glanced down at her watch. It was already late afternoon. She'd have to get back to the office to make sure the final statements and debriefing had been handled.

"He's not going anywhere tonight." The surgeon's voice was serious. "He'll be in Intensive Care until tomorrow and then we'll transfer him to a regular room."

"I need to set up a security detail."

"Not in the ICU. You can have someone outside the waiting room door, but that's the only concession I'll make. My patient isn't in any condition to escape." The surgeon turned to leave and then stopped. "What did he do?"

Grace swallowed. "He was returning a boy who'd been kidnapped. When I ordered him to stop, he reached into his pocket."

The surgeon raised an eyebrow. "Did he pull a weapon out?"

"He was resisting arrest." Grace's tone was defensive.

"I'll take that as a negative." The surgeon shook his head and left the waiting room.

Grace pulled out her phone. She'd spent enough time going over the scenario in her mind. Partlan had left them no choice. All he had to do was stop. Instead, he'd refused, and walked away. He might consider everything he'd done justified, but it was her duty to defend the law, not flaunt it. That didn't explain why her stomach was tied in knots and refused to settle.

The image of his face in the ambulance was etched in her memory.

His words would haunt her forever.

She gripped the phone tighter. She had work to do. Standing here berating herself for doing her duty wasn't getting any of it done. The debriefing of the Walters hadn't gone well, so she needed to arrange to speak to them tomorrow. After they'd had a chance to realize how lucky they were to get their son back, they'd be more likely to see how right the FBI had been. There was no place for vigilante justice in the world.

She started to dial her office number when a hand grabbed her phone away. She frowned and reached for her cell, but stopped when she saw who was standing there. It was her supervisor, Assistant Special Agent in Charge, Carter.

"Sir?" Grace raised an eyebrow. "Is there a new development?"

"That's why I'm here." Carter's eyes narrowed. "Have you listened to the news?"

She shook her head. "I've been waiting for the surgeon."

"What's the prognosis?"

"He thinks the prisoner will survive. He's in Intensive Care right now." Grace pointed at her phone. "I was just going to let the guard detail know."

"I'm glad he'll live." Carter handed her the phone. "The guards are more important now than before."

Grace had been working in the FBI too long not recognize the serious tone of Carter's voice. Something had happened while she was in the waiting room and from the look of ASAC Carter's face, it wasn't good. She straightened her shoulders and readied herself for bad news. She'd been in charge of the operation to recover the Walters' child, so she'd be the one who'd take the fall for anything that had gone wrong.

The problem was nothing had gone right since she'd been assigned the kidnapping. There was no deflecting blame in the FBI. She knew that going into this assignment. A celebrity case like this was seldom a career booster.

"What's happened?"

"Sit." Carter motioned to one of the chairs. "We have to talk."

Chapter 3

"The Walters have given a press conference."

Grace's stomach sank. "How bad is the damage?"

Carter shook his head. "It doesn't look good. According to them, you willfully thwarted the actions of a group of men they hired to find their son. Some group called aHunter4Hire. Is this true?"

"They're vigilantes and I didn't stop them from doing their own investigation." Grace fought to keep her voice low. How dare the Walters complain after all the work her team had done to find their son? "Did they happen to mention that their nanny's boyfriend was one of the men?"

"They did their best to make certain we looked like the bad guys." Carter's voice was dry. "Now we have to prove them wrong."

Grace nodded. "That should be easy enough. We took a gun from the prisoner and I'm certain he used it in other shootings."

"I've got ballistics looking into it."

"What about the men who are alive in Caliente?" Grace stood and started to pace. "Have they said anything?"

"They're refusing to speak without lawyers."

Grace snorted. "That's wise considering the evidence I had emailed to me from their laptops."

"Who sent it?"

Grace bit her lip. "The prisoner."

Carter leaned back in his chair. "That might be a problem. It'll look like he was working with us."

"I had no idea what they intended." Grace hugged her arms close to her body in an attempt to maintain self-control. "I did everything in my power to stop them from interfering with the investigation."

"You should have arrested them."

"They did nothing illegal." Grace bit back her exasperation. "Even when I told them to stay away, they would show up. If I arrested them, then I'd have to detain all the journalist who follow us because they had a lead. Partlan and his men were careful not to cross the line."

"Then how did they find the boys and kill people in the process?"

"They didn't share information with us, so I had no idea that they were looking at the Gordon brothers for the kidnapping."

"Why weren't we looking at them?"

Grace swallowed back her indignation. Her team had done everything possible to find those boys. "The Gordon's weren't identified as being at the park that day."

"Somehow this group of unknowns were able to hijack our investigation and find the kids. Explain."

"The nanny, Selena Duarte hired them." A muscle in Grace's jaw twitched. "She was familiar with these men from her days in Colombia."

"So they're mercenaries?" Carter's eyes narrowed. "What possessed you to let them have free rein?"

"I didn't sir." Grace took a deep breath. Experience had taught her that getting defensive with Carter only made things worse. She needed to take control and make this situation right. "We can only assume that they hacked into our computers. They also had the nanny feeding them information."

Carter sat back and crossed his arms. "Was the nanny involved?"

Grace shook her head. "No. It turns out one of the mercenaries was the father of Tarrin, the other boy kidnapped along with the Walters' son."

Carter pursed his lips. "And we shot one of them."

"He gave us no choice."

"Let's hope not." Carter stood. "I've already arranged for a guard this evening. You need to get back to the office and get your report to me ASAP. I'll give a press conference in the morning to repair the damage the Walters did."

Grace shifted her gun and put her phone in her jacket pocket. She pulled out her car keys and walked with Carter outside. It was going to be another night spent at the office, so she'd hit a fast food restaurant for something to eat. Not that she felt much like eating. Her stomach was still uneasy and she had to force herself to look straight ahead when she left the hospital parking lot. There was an invisible connection with Partlan. She wanted to stay there with him.

An hour later, she was sitting at her desk munching on French fries and sipping a chocolate milkshake. She had Bakker and Smythe's reports in front of her. There was nothing in them that was a surprise.

"You must be really upset." Smythe came into her office and plopped down on a chair.

Grace raised an eyebrow. "Why?"

Smythe pointed to the fry in her hand. "Junk food. You never touch the stuff unless your mind is in overload."

Grace grimaced. "We still haven't heard from ballistics about Partlan's gun. In my gut I know it was used before."

Smythe shrugged. "It doesn't matter if he's a mass killer. All the public is going to see is that we shot a man who found two kids that were kidnapped. He's a hero."

"Don't remind me." Grace leaned back in her chair and took a sip of her shake. "What's the report from Caliente? Are any of the victims talking?"

Agent Smythe snorted. "Victims. You've seen the video evidence those mercenaries sent us. They make Jack the Ripper look like a saint."

"They turn my stomach, but we have to follow the law."

Agent Bakker walked in at that moment and threw some papers on her desk. "Looks like the Caliente fiasco can be called self-defense. Forensics isn't finished, but both sides were shooting. Bullets from our prisoner's gun match a couple of slugs that were taken out of two of the victims."

"That might be enough to hold him." Grace sat forward and pulled the reports toward her. "Is there anything else?"

"We got a lead on a couple of the kids that were being held by the Caliente group. It seems they showed up at their parents' houses a few hours ago. Each was escorted by one of the mercenaries that Selina Duarte called in."

"Have we got statements from the kids?"

Bakker pointed at the papers in her hands. "They all claim that it was men called Hunters that saved them. The other men who were holding them, forced them into a hiding hole in the floor and then started to fire. It looks like self-defense."

"Damn."

Nausea rolled in her stomach. The last thing she needed was to have her team accused of shooting an innocent man, even if it looked as if he were reaching for a weapon. She'd spent too many years moving her way up the ranks of the FBI to end up at the bottom of the heap again.

Life had taught her to expect the unexpected.

It had also shown her that she was the only one who could make things right.

She went through the statements from the kids. They all said the same thing. They were being held in an underground cellar with guns aimed at them. When the Hunter had opened the trapdoor, the Caliente men had fired first. That meant everything would be explained as self-defense. As long as everyone stuck to that story, there was no way they could hold Partlan on any deaths at the clubhouse where the children were being held. Smythe was right. The man was a hero.

"How did they find the gang in Caliente?" That was the only piece that wasn't clear. Grace frowned. "They emailed us about the Gordon brothers. Did they send us anything else?"

Grace turned to her computer and booted up her email. She scrolled through the information sent to her from Caliente. There were pictures, files, and a brief note to check out the Gordon brothers, but no information about how they had found the Caliente group.

"Who interviewed the Gordon brothers?"

"I did." Bakker cleared his throat. "All they did was complain about the rough treatment they'd received at the hands of the Hunters. They were especially upset with the leader."

"Partlan." Grace pursed her lips. "It's not enough to hold him. What else did the brothers tell you?"

"They apparently sold the boys, but no names were exchanged."

"Something must have led Partlan to Caliente." Grace tapped her fingers on her desk as she flipped through the papers. Somewhere in these statements were the answers she needed.

"I found a storage unit that the brothers had and sent a team over to investigate. There was video of the brothers talking with a man. Michael's was trying to enhance it for clues."

"Is he back yet?"

Bakker shrugged. "I'll check."

When Bakker left the room, Smythe shifted in his chair. "What are you thinking?"

"The missing link must be important, or they would have taken the time to email it to us."

Grace continued to shift through Bakker's paperwork until she found the interview with the Gordon brothers. They had originally kidnapped the boys and then sold them after they'd made a successful escape with the ransom money. Partlan's mercenaries had found the brothers and retrieved the money. Bakker's report went on to describe the numerous complaints the brothers had made against Partlan, but none of them would be enough to justify holding him, especially since the Walters' press conference.

She was certain he'd broken the law.

She just needed evidence.

Bakker rushed into her office. "Michael enhanced the license plate of the car in the video. It led to a David Hendry. You'll never guess what he found when he went to speak to Mr. Hendry."

"He was handcuffed to the radiator like the Gordon brothers?" Smythe's voice was bored.

"Better." Bakker grinned. "He was dead."

"Tell me Michael ran the ballistics." Grace held her breath.

Bakker nodded. "The bullet matches the gun we took from Partlan."

"Bingo." Smythe snapped his fingers. "What does forensics say about the scene?"

"They're still processing it, but who cares. The gun matches."

Grace couldn't contain her smile. "That's good enough for now. We have grounds to arrest Partlan for suspicion of murder."

Chapter 4

Partlan wrestled his way through the fog that clouded his brain. There was a loud beeping noise near his head and his mouth was dry. He needed water and to stop that incessant noise. He tried to lift his arm to shut the racket off, but it would not move. His hand was locked in place. He forced his eyes open and saw the handcuffs holding him to the bedrail.

He sensed her near.

He scanned the room and saw her.

Agent Kelly. She had been his last thought before he lost consciousness. His heart beat in rhythm with the beeping near his ear, but he ignored it. All that mattered, was that she was here with him. Her golden hair was tied away from her face, not a strand out of place. She was sitting with her hands clasped in her lap and a notebook and pen ready. He wanted to shout for joy. Instead, he said the one thing most important to him at that moment.

"Water."

Agent Kelly frowned. "I don't know if you should have liquids."

"Water." Partlan did not care if it was permitted. His throat was as dry as the desert winds on Beligia.

Agent Kelly looked over her shoulder and then picked up a glass of water. It had a straw and she held it up to Partlan. He took a sip and then another until the glass was empty. He leaned back against his pillow and watched as the FBI agent refilled the glass. When she held it up to him, he shook his head.

As much as he craved her nearness, he could not take another sip.

"Why are you here?"

"I still have questions for you." Agent Kelly pulled her chair closer to the bed and sat. "What did you do to David Hendry?"

Partlan grimaced as he fought to remember. The medicine they had given him was wreaking havoc on his thinking and movement. The last thing he recalled was being in the ambulance and looking at Agent Kelly. He knew he had been dying, so why was he still here?

"How come I am alive?"

"Your heart stopped in the ambulance." There was a flicker of emotion that crossed Agent Kelly's face. "They brought you back."

"That would explain it." Partlan's words faded out.

"What?"

"I did not expect to wake." Partlan shook his hand that was cuffed to the bed. "Or to be forced to face your interrogation."

"I only need a few things clarified." Her voice was defensive. "I'm sorry about the shooting. Bakker thought you were reaching for a weapon."

"I would never hurt a woman." Partlan's gaze was steady. "It is forbidden and against the code I live by."

"I'm your enemy."

Partlan shook his head. "You could never be that."

A wary look came into her eyes. "I don't understand you."

"It is very simple. There is a connection between us."

She inhaled a sharp breath. "I have arrested you. That is the only connection we have."

He looked at her for a few seconds before answering. "It is as you wish. I will answer your questions now."

"David Hendry?"

Partlan had almost forgotten Hendry. He was the man who had brokered the sale of the boys. Hendry had enjoyed hurting children and had refused to help his team find Gates and Tarrin. He had broken the Sacred Code that all Hunters lived by. The first rule stated no harm was to come to women or children. Execution was the penalty for breaking the code. Partlan felt no remorse in the man's death.

"He is not my concern." Partlan had learned not to admit anything to police officers because it would be twisted by their laws. "The man had no honor. He abused and sold children. He had to die."

"So you killed him."

"He reached for my gun and when I resisted, he was shot." Partlan's jaw clenched. "Honor demanded that he die."

"Are you nuts?" Agent Kelly jumped up from her chair and started pacing. "We could have learned more about his network if he were alive. Now all of those monsters will go free."

"We left his computer for you."

"That's encrypted." She threw her arms up in the air. "You may have gotten the children back alive, but the real criminals will go free."

"That is why it is best to kill them."

She opened and shut her mouth before sitting down again. "You can't be serious."

"A Hunter does not lie."

"So you're saying that you shot Hendry in self-defense."

"The man was an abomination. If he had not reached for the gun, I would still have killed him."

"I'm only interested in what actually happened. Not what you wanted to do."

"He deserved to die." Partlan watched Agent Kelly's eyes narrow. "You do not like my words, but you cannot deny that it is more logical than letting him live."

"That is for the courts to decide."

"What if they had let him go free?"

"Then it is my job to uphold their decision."

"So you understand honor." His voice held a note of satisfaction.

Finally, common ground. Partlan had been fighting the need to be with this woman since they had started their investigation into the kidnapping. It was illogical and dangerous to be near her. Already he had been shot and was lying in this hospital without defenses. It made no sense, but he could not stop the joy that filled his heart when he spoke with her.

He needed to keep her near.

Everything else was forgotten.

"I have always lived by honor, which is more than I could say about the men I've met."

Partlan watched the shadows cross her face.

Pain, anger, and resentment were evident.

"Men have hurt you." It was a statement. Her whole demeanor told him it was true.

Agent Kelly turned her head away. "We're not talking about me."

"I am unused to conversing with women." Partlan's tone was apologetic. "I did not mean to offend you."

Agent Kelly's eyes sparked fire. "Don't try that one on me."

Partlan frowned. "Try what?"

"There's no way a guy who looks like you isn't familiar with the opposite sex. All you have to do is snap your fingers and you can get any woman you want."

"It is forbidden for a Hunter to mate."

Her eyes widened. "I thought you didn't lie."

"It is the truth." Partlan sat up higher on his pillow. "I am a warrior. We do not have mates."

"Why, because it would interfere with your thinking?" Her voice was sarcastic.

"Hunters mate only once. Our bond with our mates is strong enough that we will do anything to protect them, even disobey our orders."

"So you can't fight if you have a mate?" She rolled her eyes. "That sounds archaic. No woman wants to think of herself as a man's mate."

"How is your concept of marriage different?"

"I didn't say I agreed with that either." Agent Kelly crossed her arms over her chest. "Marriage is just a piece of paper."

"There is no paper involved with a Hunter and his mate. It is a bonding that will last a lifetime."

"No man stays around that long."

"A Hunter does."

Agent Kelly snorted. "Enough talk about fairy tales. They don't exist. What I need from you is your statement about David Hendry, the Gordon brothers, and what happened in Caliente."

"We found the brothers by checking the photos of the other photographers that had been at the park that day. We were suspicious after the ransom drop. It was obvious that one of the paparazzi was involved." Partlan's voice was bored. They had followed the usual steps of elimination before approaching the Gordon brothers. It was something the FBI should have done themselves.

"When we found the brothers, they were getting ready to leave the country. They had the ransom money."

"You should have called the FBI at that point." Agent Kelly looked up from the pad she had been scribbling on.

"Why? I have dealt with many takings, or as you call them, kidnappings. I am experienced with finding people. That is what Hunters do."

"I've never heard of mercenaries rescuing people." A muscle clenched in agent Kelly's jaw. "Who else have you worked for?"

"I worked for the Kaladin."

"I've never heard of them." She started writing again. After a few seconds, she looked up. "You can continue with your version of the kidnapping."

"The Gordon brothers told us they sold the boys. They did not exchange names with the buyer, but made the deal at their storage unit. We left them handcuffed at their house because Selina asked us to let them live."

Partlan bit back the disgust he had felt at leaving the brothers alive. His instinct was to kill them for what they had done. They had no honor, and even though they were cowards, keeping them alive would not change who they were. To kidnap young children because you were angry, and then to sell them once you had extorted money, were not the actions of reasonable men. At their core, they were damaged.

"You sound disappointed. Selena showed great presence of mind." Agent Kelly tried to hide her grin. "At least you won't be charged with their murder."

"These men will harm again."

"Not in prison." Agent Kelly looked up from her pad. "They will be put away for the rest of their lives because of the kidnapping."

"If your courts find them guilty." Partlan clenched his hands into fists. "I have heard that your justice is not always fair."

"Everyone is equal under the law."

The FBI agent spoke by rote, but she didn't' fool Partlan. He sensed her ambivalence. She might defend the law, but she was not blind to its weaknesses. Partlan's respect for the agent increased.

"You do not sound satisfied with your legal system."

Agent Kelly straightened her shoulders. "I know some try to manipulate it. The Walters are trying to do that for you right now."

"I did not ask them to do anything." Partlan shifted on the bed. "I said we would bring their son back because he had been taken with Tarrin."

"But Tarrin meant more to you than Gates."

"Rescuing both boys was important." Partlan's voice held a mild reprove. "I will not apologize about my connection with Tarrin. His father is a Hunter, and that makes Tarrin a brother."

The agent lifted an eyebrow and gave Partlan a steely stare. "Why didn't you tell us that Catal was his father?"

"We did not know."

"I find that hard to believe. If you did the math, you would have been able to backtrack when Catal and Selena had been an item. It doesn't take a genius to figure out he was probably the father."

Partlan clenched his jaw. "Catal claimed Selena as his mate. We are sworn to protect a fellow Hunter's mate and children. The parentage of the children does not matter to us."

"She denied knowing who the father was." Agent Kelly's grip on her pencil tightened. "It was stupid of me not to realize it would have been one of the men she called in for help."

"We did not make the connection either." Partlan forced his gaze away from the agent.

"I don't understand." Her voice held confusion. "You were closest to Catal. Surely he knew?"

Partlan looked back. Her face was tilted and there was a furrow between her eyes. For a second, he longed to hold her and kiss away her worries. She would not allow that, so instead he would tell her a truth about himself.

"Until Catal found out he had a son, we did not think we could father children."

Her eyes widened. "That's another one of your lies. Why would a group of men believe they were sterile?"

"Where I come from, we do not have children." Despite the ache in his head, Partlan lifted his chin. "We were bred to be warriors, not to father children."

"Bred?" Agent Kelly's head jerked back. "That sounds like something out of a science fiction book. You're good at fighting. That's the only reason men became mercenaries."

"Not Hunters. We are genetically modified to be warriors, and from our first breath to our last, we protect."

"Now I know you're not telling the truth." Agent Kelly crossed her arms over her legs, letting her writing pad tangle over the edge of her lap. "Despite what you see in the movies, science is not that advanced on Earth."

"I did not say I came from Earth. I am from Cygnus."

Partlan waited for her reaction. It was a risk telling her, but he had to try to convince her to let him go free. This planet was not friendly to aliens. Since they had crash landed almost a year ago, they had hid from the authorities. As a prisoner, he would not be able to protect himself or her, if threats were made.

He had not had time to contact Ardal, the leader of their unit either. His last mind connection had been when he was shot. Ardal needed to know what had happened to him. He would have to check in soon so that he would know how to proceed.

"You said you didn't lie." Agent Kelly shook her head. "Let's just look at the facts of the kidnapping for now."

"I have told you the truth. It is your decision whether to believe or not." Partlan tried to move his arm, but the handcuffs reminded him of his restraints. "Are these necessary?"

"You're the one who unarmed my agents at the Walters' house. I'm not taking a chance that you'll escape again."

"It will not prevent me from leaving."

"You're in no condition to run." Agent Kelly picked up her pencil. "How did you find Hendry?"

"He met the Gordon brothers at the storage locker. It was a matter of identifying the car and getting his address from his license."

"And shooting him." The agent's eyebrow rose. "Which you claim was in self-defense."

"It was."

"Continue."

"Hendry told us that the boys were put on a transport truck, but he only saw the word Diamond. We found the name of a Diamond Haulage on his emails and proceeded from there."

"You took a chance with that one."

Partlan shrugged. "We followed the wrong truck at first. It did not prevent us from reaching the boys in time."

"So now we get to the interesting part. The shootout in Caliente."

"They came out of the building with shotguns." Partlan's voice was matter of fact. "We had no choice. The children were being held there."

"You could have called me." Agent Kelly flipped her notebook shut. "I would have had an armed unit there within the hour."

"Children's lives were at risk. It is not our practice to wait."

Partlan shut his eyes as a wave of weakness descended. His words seemed to be tied up in his tongue. He tried to continue speaking, but nothing came out. Exhaustion took over and he was powerless to control his body. He fell into a deep sleep.

How long he slept he did not know, but the sun was setting low in the sky when he awoke. Agent Kelly was still in the room. She was curled up in one of the chairs sleeping. She was using her coat as a blanket, and her arm for a pillow. In slumber, she looked even more beautiful.

Partlan inhaled an awed breath.

He could feel the steady beat of her heart.

His beat in unison. Her breathing was faint, but he strained his ears and mind to be certain she was content. Her face was relaxed and the stern lines around her mouth and eyes were gone. It was the first time he had seen her at peace. His heart soared with happiness. It was a new emotion for him.

He wanted to reach out and touch her; to brush the hair away from her eyes. Never had he noticed a woman before. He sent her a wave of calm and then leaned back to mind connect with his unit.

He reached out for Ardal, his leader. *"It is Partlan. I am still in Beverly Hills."*

"What happened?" Ardal's voice was clear in his mind.

"Agent Bakker shot me when I was trying to leave. Agent Kelly has arrested me and is holding me at the hospital."

"Can you escape?"

"If necessary. I am handcuffed to the bed, but these restraints will not last long."

"Good. I am sending men to you."

"I should warn you of one other development."

"Continue."

"I am certain that Agent Kelly is my pair bond."

Chapter 5

A sharp pain shot through Partlan's shoulder as he twisted the handcuffs back and forth. The metal was bending and soon it would be weak enough for him to break it. He clenched his jaw and twisted again. Pain was meant to be endured. Training and combat had taught him that there were worse things.

The constant smell of antiseptic surrounded him. It was the second day after the shooting and he was anxious to leave the dull green, institutional walls that surrounded him. Humans might find it comforting to be in such a sterile environment, but he found it stifling. He might as well be locked away in a prison cell.

He gave his wrist another twist.

The machine at the head of the bed began to beep faster and footsteps could be heard in the corridor. He took a deep breath and steadied his heart until the noise subsided. The door pushed open and a nurse moved toward him. She checked the monitor and then the dressing on his chest.

"The doctor will be in soon." She adjusted one of the leads to his chest and then moved to inspect his arm where the IV had been inserted. "He's doing rounds right now."

She followed the tubing of his IV to the pump and then pushed a few buttons before turning to him with a smile. She was young and beautiful and her brown eyes were soft as they settled on him. Partlan felt no stirring of interest or attraction. It was as it had always been. In thirty-three years the only woman who had excited him was Agent Kelly.

"Is there anything you need?" The nurse picked up the water jug from his side table and filled it at the sink.

Partlan's eyes followed her movements. "I am fine."

At that moment the doctor walked in.

"I would have to agree." The doctor flipped through paper on his chart. "It's amazing. Your lab results are almost perfect."

The doctor put the chart down on the bed beside him and then removed the dressing on his chest. "Any pain?"

Partlan shook his head. "I am anxious to leave."

The doctor took a closer look at the exposed wound. "Remarkable."

"What?" The voice of Agent Kelly echoed in the small hospital room.

"My patient has extraordinary restorative powers. I've never seen anything like it in all my years of surgery. It's almost completely healed." The doctor stepped away and motioned to the nurse. "You can redress this."

Agent Kelly moved closer to the bed. A surge of joy moved through Partlan as his eyes lingered on the tall, beautiful agent. She was dressed as usual, in a dark baggy pant suit with her hair dragged back behind her head in a tight bun. She was frowning and he fought the urge to pull her into his arms and comfort her. His only desire was that she be happy.

"When can he be released?"

"Normally I'd say in a week, but at this rate, he should be good to go in a day or two." The doctor stepped back to let the nurse cleanse the wound.

"Good." Agent Kelly's eyes skittered away from his bruised and reddened chest. "My supervisor wants him in custody."

"I said he could go home, not to prison." The doctor picked up the chart from the bed. "Unless he's going to a hospital facility in jail, he'd be better off here."

"He needs to come with me for further questioning."

The nurse finished with her work and moved away. Partlan flexed his chest muscles. The new bandage held. He nodded at the nurse and then turned his attention back to Agent Kelly. Her brow was furrowed and her face reddened.

"He needs rest." The doctor clasped the chart close to his chest and held the door open for the nurse to pass through. "I'm not releasing him just because you want him for interrogation."

The doctor left the room.

Silence followed him.

Partlan cleared his throat. "I will go with you now, if you wish."

Agent Kelly shook her head and threw herself down in the chair beside the bed. "I have to follow the doctor's orders. I can't move you until he releases you, or your lawyer might use that against us in court."

"I do not have a lawyer."

Partlan leaned back on his pillows. A sense of peace enveloped him. Agent Kelly had brought the sunshine in with her. He might be locked to a bed and facing custody, but that did not matter. All he cared about was being near to her.

"You have the right to have a lawyer appointed to you."

"What will they do?"

"Protect you and make certain you don't incriminate yourself." Agent Kelly pulled her small pad out of her pocket.

"I trust you."

"You shouldn't." Agent Kelly's eyes avoided his. "I am trying to have you arrested in the shooting of David Hendry."

"Have your experts not explained what happened?"

Partlan's voice was devoid of emotion. As connected as he was to Agent Kelly, he would not deny who he was. He was a warrior sworn to protect. David Hendry would have died at his hands even if he had not struggled with Partlan for the gun. There were no second chances when the lives of women or children were threatened or damaged.

"Yes." Agent Kelly sounded disappointed. "The forensics confirm what you told me. You're lucky."

"Luck had nothing to do with it. I am a skilled warrior."

"You're pretty sure of yourself." The FBI agent sat up in her chair and clicked her pen open. "Explain what happened at Caliente again."

"As you wish."

Partlan leaned back and started to relate the story of the capture of the child traffickers and the rescue of their captives again. As he spoke, he twisted his handcuff until the metal bent with ease. Soon he would be free and then he would have no choice. He would escape. It would be easier if he left before being taken to the FBI headquarters.

When he had finished relating the story, Agent Kelly clicked her pen a couple of times. "Tell me about the judge."

"Catal killed him." Partlan shrugged. "The judge came after him with a gun and shot at Catal and his family. The man deserved to die."

"It seems you always have a reason to kill people." Agent Kelly sat forward in her chair. "Do you leave anyone alive?"

"There would be no honor in killing innocent people."

"So you recognize that some people are innocent." She emphasized the word innocent with sarcasm.

Partlan tilted his head. "We protect. That means only those causing harm will be killed."

Agent Kelly exhaled a loud breath. "There is no deviation from that? Is there no grey in your universe?"

"Grey is a color." Partlan frowned. "What has that to do with honor?"

"Black and white, right and wrong." Kelly's voice rose in exasperation. "You can't tell me you've never heard the term grey being used for middle ground."

"Your language is still unclear to me. Where I am from, we do not use words to mean more than one thing."

"Unbelievable." Agent Kelly closed her notebook. "So there is no change in your story?"

"Why would I alter the truth?"

Partlan sensed her frustration, but he did not understand how he could make things better for her. He could not lie. A Hunter did not dishonor himself in such a way. The men they had killed at Caliente had shot first. He would have killed them whether they attacked or not.

"We did leave some alive." Partlan's voice was conciliatory.

"That's a blessing I suppose." Agent Kelly sighed. "We're interrogating them now, but they refuse to talk and have lawyered up. They're a pretty well connected lot."

"We should have killed them."

Agent Kelly rolled her eyes. "I'm surprised you didn't. What stopped you?"

"Selena asked us to let them live."

"That's the second time you listened to her. Why?"

"She is a woman. We obey."

Agent Kelly's eyes widened and she sat back in her chair. She opened her mouth to speak and then shut it. It made no sense to Partlan why she would be surprised, but he had learned that what was normal on Cygnus, was not true on Earth. He waited for her to speak.

"Are you telling me that if I told you to do something, you would?"

"As long as it did not interfere with your safety." Partlan's tone was firm. "I have learned that women on Earth are not used to ruling and sometimes make decisions that can harm them."

"So you're sticking to your story about not being from Earth?" Agent Kelly's voice held disbelief.

"I am from Cygnus."

The FBI agent laughed. "I get it. You're trying for an insanity plea. It won't work."

"I am sane. Why would I suggest otherwise?"

"To get away with murder." Agent Kelly grinned. "It's brilliant. I've never heard of anyone who believes they're an alien. Lots have said they've seen or heard aliens, though."

"I do not claim anything." Partlan refused to be angered by her ridicule. Being defensive would not convince her of who he was. "I am telling you the truth."

"Why don't you just announce it over the loudspeaker? That way everyone will hear and you can bring them to your defense in court."

"It is dangerous to let people know we are not from this planet."

"So all of your men are from outer space?"

She covered her mouth with her hand, but Partlan sensed her amusement. It was better that she did not believe. The attraction he felt to her was not lessening. It was growing every second he spent with her, and if he ever hoped to complete the pair bond, she must understand that he was not the same as a human man. He had to be honest with Agent Kelly.

"We crash landed on your planet almost one year ago."

"I thought Catal was Tarrin's father." Agent Kelly did not bother to hide her smirk. "That blows your story right there."

"Catal was stranded on the planet when he was a child." Partlan twisted the handcuff again. "He and others from his craft survived by hiring out as mercenaries. Our leader, Ardal, agreed to complete their training as Hunters and they have since joined our unit."

Agent Kelly rolled her eyes. "How many of you are there?"

"We number over one hundred."

"That's a lot of aliens." Her tone was condescending. "Don't you think our government would have let us know about that many extraterrestrials living on our planet?"

"When we first crashed, we were hunted down. Our leader and his mate were captured and escaped. Your government is aware of our existence."

"That's pretty convenient." Agent Kelly pushed up from her chair. "I'm not biting. You'll have to do better than that to get out of the mess you're in. As it stands, I could build a case against you for obstruction of justice, at the very least."

"I ensured justice was done." Partlan did not hide his confusion. "Your laws make no sense."

She put her pen and pad into her pocket. "You are not law enforcement. Your interference caused people to die." She leaned closer to him. "Nobody will buy the alien thing either, so I wouldn't bother trying it on someone else."

"You are the only one I would tell." Partlan cleared his throat. "It is important for honesty between us."

"Why is that?" Agent Kelly rapped a finger on his bedrail. "Are you hoping to plea bargain this down to a misdemeanor?"

"Your words make no sense to me." Partlan lowered his voice. "I have told you this truth because we are connected."

Agent Kelly's eyes widened. "Are you trying to seduce me in the hope that I'll drop the charges?"

"I do not seduce women." Partlan's tone was cold.

"Good." Agent Kelly straightened her shoulders. "It won't work. I swore off men years ago. The only thing that is important to me is the law."

She turned to leave, but a knock at the door stopped her. Partlan glanced over her shoulder and saw two men walk in and shut the door behind them. They were about five feet in height and both were wearing long black overcoats over black suits. Their eyes were shaded by dark sunglasses perched on tiny noses. Black fedora-like hats covered their heads.

"Can I help you?" Agent Kelly turned to walk toward them.

Partlan grabbed her hand. When she tried to twist away, he held firm. It was not the clothes they wore that upset him. It was the all too familiar features of pale, hairless skin and black eyes that peered through the sunglasses. Partlan's nose twitched at the faint odor of plastic and salt.

He forced his heartbeat to slow and twisted the handcuff with the full force of his muscles. It broke with a clatter that made Agent Kelly look back at him with a frown. He did not care. Now was not the time for secrecy. He had to get both of them away from these men.

They were the scourge of the Cygnus galaxy; one that he had spent most of his military career fighting.

They were not human.

They were Albireons.

Chapter 6

"We have come to see the man the Walters called a hero."

"Partlan?" Agent Kelly frowned. "He's my prisoner and visitors are forbidden. How did you get past the guard outside?"

"No one there." He sounded like a computer speaking.

"Who are you guys?" She tried to move toward them, but Partlan held her arm.

"It is wrong that they are here." Partlan tugged on her arm. "We need to leave."

Confusion twisted her thinking. First, Partlan tries to tell her he's an alien, and now these two weirdoes show up. She was the person in control here. She lifted her chin and glared at the intruders. Large hypnotic eyes focused on her. A wave of dizziness swept through her. She grasped the bedrail to keep herself from falling.

"Do not look them in the eye," Partlan commanded.

She shook her head and broke contact.

Nausea churned in her stomach.

"Do you know them?" Her voice was a low whisper.

"They are Albireons. They are not from this planet."

She turned to face Partlan. "You can't be serious. They look strange enough to be aliens, but why would they come here?"

"I told you I was not safe on Earth." Partlan pulled the IV from his arm.

"You must stay put." The statement was in a monotone. "There are others coming."

"That is what I was afraid of." Partlan pushed his covers off. "Where are my clothes?"

It took Grace a second to realize that Partlan was out of bed. She went to stop him, but he stepped past her and opened the small closet door beside the bed. He found the jeans and black, military-style boots that he had been wearing when he was brought into the hospital. He put the clothes on and then rummaged for a shirt, but that had been cut off his body and thrown away. He ripped the bottom of his hospital gown off and tucked it into his pants.

"We need to leave."

One of the strangers reached a hand out for her. Partlan struck it away and pushed her behind him. She found herself staring at his back. This was crazy. She was the trained agent and she wasn't going to allow anyone to take Partlan. She still needed him to answer her questions.

"You cannot run." The strange mechanical voice stated. "The others will be here in short time."

"We are leaving."

Partlan picked one of the men up by the neck and shook him. His hat and sunglasses fell off. They had no eyebrows or eyelashes.

The man had a slit for a mouth, and used makeup to create the illusion of lips. When he spoke, his mouth didn't move. She forced back her panic. There was a logical explanation for who these guys were and it wasn't that they were from another planet. She stretched a hand out to stop Partlan, but he ignored it. He threw the man to the ground and reach for his partner.

"Stop this." Her words caught in her throat. That's when she remembered her gun. She reached under her jacket and pulled it out from her holster and took off the safety. She held the gun close to her body and took a step back.

"Put him down." She used her most authoritative tone.

Partlan let go.

The man dropped with a loud thud. She pointed her gun at the intruders on the floor. "Now I want the two of you to back up against the far wall."

One man reached an arm out at her. Her gun started to wobble in her hand. She brought her other hand up to hold it tighter, but the pistol's vibrations were so strong that her teeth were rattling in her mouth. Partlan reached over and clasped her hands together. The shaking movement settled down.

"Your powers are not enough." Partlan's voice was a hiss. "You should not be on this planet."

"We know what you are capable of, Hunter." One of the men dressed in black stood. "We have sent for reinforcements."

Partlan took the gun from her and pushed it into his waistband. There was a numbing tingle in her hands and she shook them in an effort to restore sensation. It was as if there had been an invisible power source directed at her gun. That was impossible. She was current on all the latest weapons and she hadn't read of any that could cause an object to shake.

Partlan reached for her arm. "We need to leave."

Grace pulled away. "Let me call headquarters. I'll have these men arrested for interfering with a federal case."

"You stay." The intruders were both standing now.

"No." Partlan pushed the bedside tray at the men. It crashed into them. While they were trying to get out from under it, Partlan pulled her close and ran out of the room. He grabbed a chair from the hallway and wedged it under the door handle. One of the nurses yelled at him to stop, but they ran past her before she could get reinforcements. There was a cleaning cart in the hallway and Partlan grabbed a broom from it. Grace assumed that he was going to use it as a weapon.

"What did they do with the guard?"

Partlan darted toward the stairs. He glanced up at the camera on the wall and used the broom handle to angle it higher down the hall. Then, he pushed her through the door to the emergency escape. They ran down the three flights of stairs. At each level, he pushed the door open a few inches and used the broom handle to reposition the camera.

Grace waited for him. It was crazy to be running, but without knowing what had happened to her security officer, she didn't want to take any chances. They didn't stop on the ground floor, but continued down to the basement level. Before stepping through the door, he pushed the camera so that it was turned in the opposite direction. They inched along the grey cement walls until they reached a door marked mechanical room. Partlan tried the handle, but it was locked.

He rested his head against the door. "Do you have any instruments to unlock this?"

"I'm not breaking the law." Grace crossed her arms over her chest.

Partlan's breath was coming in gasps. "It is either us or them. If Albireons can walk openly on this planet, then they already have control. We need to get back to my unit. That is our only hope of safety."

"Why are you so worried about those men? Between the two of us, we could have wrestled them to the ground and handcuffed them."

"You saw their powers." Partlan turned away from the door and looked at her. "They were able to force you to do what you did not desire."

A shiver ran through Grace. She'd become dizzy when she'd looked at them, but that could happen to anyone. The incident with the gun wasn't as easily explained. Her hand had shook uncontrollably. Then, there was their appearance. They hadn't looked like any human she'd ever seen before.

"What do you know about them?" She wasn't ready to believe they were aliens, but Partlan's answers might give her a clue as to why they were chasing them.

"I was taken prisoner by Albireons during the Kepler Insurrections." Partlan's voice was barely a whisper. "I've been trained to withstand torture and pain, but what they did was worse."

"How can anything be worse?" Grace's spoke in a hushed tone.

"They invade your mind and then they assault your body." Partlan gazed down at her. "There is no escaping their insidious tentacles of exploration. That's how they conquer. They understand how a race thinks and they replicate their genome."

"Are you suggesting this is why they are on Earth?"

"Probably." Partlan's voice held a faint tremor. "It is imperative that we escape them. I cannot ensure your safety otherwise."

"I can take care of myself." Grace's tone was hard-edged. "Whether I believe what you say about those men or not, you're my prisoner. I won't let them take you."

She started rooting through her pockets. "Do you know how insane you sound? You're still recovering from major surgery. Running around is not doing you any good. I'm FBI and perfectly capable of handling this situation."

"You do not understand the menace of the Albireons. They are the locust of the universe. They swarm and take over planets at will."

Grace shook her head. "Does it look like someone has taken over this planet?"

"They do not attack with weapons."

Grace patted her hair and pulled out a couple of bobby pins. "So they sneak up on us and steal our minds and bodies. That sounds like a movie I once saw."

Partlan took the pins and twisted them open before inserting them in the lock. He worked the mechanism for a few seconds and turned the knob when a faint click sounded. The door opened. He pushed her in and locked the door behind them.

"There is no sneaking with them. They come bearing gifts and then attack when least expected. By then, it is too late because they have already broken through the planet's defenses."

"First the movies and now Greek mythology." Grace straightened her shoulders. "I need to contact my office. They'll send somebody to help."

Partlan stopped and looked at her for a few seconds before nodding. "I will contact my unit. They have to be made aware. We need to continue moving."

Grace pulled out her phone and dialed the office. It was only then that she realized what Partlan had said. If he contacted his fellow mercenaries on her cell phone, then she'd have a way to track them down.

"You can use my phone."

Partlan took her arm and moved through the labyrinth of rusty equipment and pipes. "I have already sent my message."

She stopped moving, but Partlan urged her to continue walking.

How had he contacted them?

She started to ask when the line was picked up at the other end. It was Bakker.

"This is Kelly. I'm at the hospital." She struggled for breath as Partlan kept her moving at a fast pace. "Two strange men showed up here and the guard I had posted outside Partlan's room is missing."

Bakker cleared his throat. "There have been some developments with the case. Apparently our friend's arrest has caught the attention of an agency that's way above our pay grade."

Partlan pulled her in close to him as they approached a junction in the maze of hallways. Her heart stuttered to a stop and then started to pound at a frantic rate. She looked up at him for a second and was lost in his dark eyes. Her breath caught in her throat and she forced herself to look away. This man was her responsibility. She would do her job and bring him to headquarters no matter how he made her feel.

"Have our orders changed?"

"We're supposed to hand him over."

"We have jurisdiction." Grace wanted to stamp her foot. "We captured him."

"I know." Bakker lowered his voice. "I don't trust these guys. They're probably monitoring your call right now. They're very secretive. It wouldn't surprise me if they were Black Ops."

"Are they still there?"

"They took off the minute your call came in."

"They're tracking me." Grace almost threw the phone away, but then her training kicked in. "I'll give them something to find. I'm bringing the prisoner in, but not to hand him over. There's something strange going on here and I mean to get to the bottom of it."

"Good luck."

Grace cut the call.

She glanced at the tunnels on either side of them. There was no end in sight. Dirt and grime lined the dingy, concrete block walls and the smell of oil and gasoline permeated every surface. They were on a small walkway that led from the door to this junction. There was no indication as to what direction would be the quickest one to safety.

"How long do these pipes and tunnels go for?"

Partlan shrugged as he edged around the corner. "They will lead to the outside eventually."

"Can you get us out of the hospital?" Grace started to dial another number on her phone.

Partlan took the right branch. "That was my plan."

"I don't know who you angered, but there is more than one agency looking for you. They have a lock on my phone." Grace waited until her call was answered by a recording, then she tucked the phone up behind the brace of one of the large pipes that led down the opposite tunnel.

"What are you doing?"

"I'm leaving them a trail to follow." Grace brushed her hands on the back of her pants.

"What happens when the call ends?"

"It won't be answered." Grace grinned. "I called the FBI information number. It's one of those automated answering lines. It will be at least an hour before that call is disconnected or an operator answers."

Partlan nodded. "We have no time to waste. The security cameras already know we took the stairs. When they don't find us coming out of the building, they will know we detoured."

"And the GPS in my cell will lead them here."

There was the loud banging behind them. Someone was trying to get into the mechanical room's locked door. There was no time to waste. Grace ran beside Partlan. The corridor they were in seemed to go on forever. All of her years of running and physical training were no match against Partlan. The man was a machine.

She sagged against a wall. "I need to take a breath."

Partlan nodded. "I will see what is ahead. Stay here."

"You're not going to try and escape?"

"I give you my word, I will come back. I cannot leave you, especially in a dangerous situation."

Grace slid down the wall and sat with her knees against her chest. It took several minutes before her breathing steadied and then she leaned her head against the damp basement wall. It was insane to continue running, but she wanted to take Partlan into headquarters herself. Those strange men back in his room had scared her. She shuddered when she remembered the effect their eyes had on her. There was no way she was going to hand Partlan over to them. It was her responsibility to keep him safe and she intended to do her job.

She didn't believe that they were aliens. She refused to give credence to such a ludicrous story, but whatever agency they worked for, she didn't trust them. She stood and was about to head off in the direction that Partlan had taken, when he returned.

"I have found a way to escape." Partlan pointed down the corridor. "We must hurry."

"Will they be able to follow us?" Grace jogged beside him.

"There is only one camera and I have already redirected it. We will not be seen. Once we are in place, they will not be able to follow us."

"What did you find?" Grace stumbled.

"The door is up ahead." Partlan offered her a hand. "You will be able to rest soon."

True to his word, there was an exit a hundred feet down the corridor. Partlan motioned her to stop while he opened the door a crack. He surveyed the area and then reached for her arm. The door opened into another hallway. There was an incline that leveled off at the top.

"Stay close to the wall. We will duck under the camera and make our way up the ramp."

Grace glanced in the direction that Partlan wanted her to go and nodded. Dodging surveillance was their best option. She followed close behind, stopping when he did, and moving when he motioned her. They made it up the ramp area and into a loading zone. He kept them close to the wall.

"We will leave the hospital on one of the vehicles picking up from here."

"Don't you mean deliveries?"

"They do not drop off here." Partlan pointed to a row of long boxes against the wall. The boxes were black and rested on a type of wheeled cart. "There are no cameras."

They edged over to where three cases were lined up together.

A shiver raced up Grace's spine as a premonition of Partlan's plan took hold in her brain.

"What's in there?" She fought to control the tremor in her voice. She was a federal agent, a woman in charge, not someone who was ruled by their fears. She shut her eyes for a brief second while Partlan lifted the lid and then she looked down.

The body of an elderly man wrapped in a sheet stared back at her.

"We can get into the containers and wait." He was matter of fact.

"You want me to hide in a coffin with a dead body?" Her voice vibrated with terror.

Memories of a dark, airless prison rushed at her. Her heart raced. Beads of sweat formed on her forehead and she inhaled a shaky breath as she fought for control. She'd pushed the horrible experiences from her mind and vowed never to be that helpless again. It didn't matter that her life was in jeopardy or that she was an adult. Some things never left you.

"I can't do it."

Chapter 7

Terror shone from her eyes.

Partlan sensed she was paralyzed by it.

He couldn't let the fear overwhelm her, so he opened the container next to them and carried the body of the old man to it. That left the box in front of them empty. He motioned for her to get in. A shudder went through Agent Kelly's body. Partlan did not want to cause her discomfort, but they had men pursuing them and time was running out.

"Is there no other way?" Her voice shook.

"I looked outside and there is no vehicle that we can hide in. This is our best chance to escape this place unseen."

Partlan took her arm and coaxed her toward the container. He needed to find a way to convince her to push past her fear. The threat of the Albireons was more serious than being captured by the FBI. He could escape from law enforcement, but he was not sure what power the Albireons had on this planet.

"Once we are free, I will go wherever you want me to." His words were a promise.

"You won't break your word?" Agent Kelly lifted one trembling leg into the box.

"A Hunter's word is a vow."

"And you never break your oath, right? Because other men do." Her hand gripped the edge of the coffin.

"I am not like other men."

"I swore I would never rely on another man." She bit her lower lip and then took a deep breath. "Don't make me regret trusting you."

She climbed into the container and then looked back up at him. "I'm afraid of the dark." Her voice was a low plea.

Partlan's chest tightened at her entreaty. Her fear was real and he couldn't ignore it. If all she needed from him was reassurance, then he would give her what she wanted. He pulled her gun out of his waistband and placed it in her hands. He hid the broom he carried in the other box and then checked that everything was in place before he climbed in.

"You will not be alone." His voice was soft with reassurance. "If you get overwhelmed and need to leave, I can get us out of here."

He closed the lid and then twisted his large body so he lay beside her. She pushed over to the side and he gathered her closer to him. She was shivering uncontrollably. He rubbed a hand over her back and moved his leg so she could rest on top of him. He sent her calm and soothing energy. Her heart beat and breathing slowed and after a few minutes her shivers stopped.

"How long do we have to be here?"

"As long as it takes. Remember, you are not trapped. Relax."

"How can it not affect you?" Her whisper was filled with reproach.

"I have been trained since I was a baby to deal with fear and pain."

"Nobody trains a baby."

"When I started to walk, that is when the training began."

Partlan's voice was devoid of emotion. His life and training were not something he reflected on. He accepted that his breeding meant that he was destined to fight and die. He did not question the method or the means. He did what was necessary to survive and at this moment, he needed to keep Agent Kelly safe.

The Albireons might have come for him, but they would not rest until they had captured both of them. He understood how their minds worked. Agent Kelly had refused to hand him over. She had stood in their way and they would never forget that. They sought complete control, even if they disguised it as assistance. Once Agent Kelly had questioned their authority, her fate had been sealed. She might not know it, but she was in the same danger he was, perhaps worse.

A Hunter was of use to Albireons.

A human was dispensable.

His arm tightened about her. He had to protect her, no matter what the cost. She was his pair bond. If he had any doubts, just holding her near, dispelled them. He was complete and at peace. There would be no greater joy than being able to be by her side for the rest of his life.

He had seen the look of adoration in the eyes of Ardal, his leader, when he looked at Fiona, his mate. Niail and Catal both gazed on their mates in the same way. Now he understood. It was more than just the physical reaction of having her near. It was a complete connection on every level.

Her essence surrounded and embraced him.

He desired to know everything about her.

"Your fear is easing." Partlan kept his voice low.

"Yes." Agent Kelly cleared her throat. "My brother locked me in the closet when I was a young girl. He was supposed to babysit me and he left me there during the day when my mother was working."

"So now you avoid small spaces."

"And the dark." She heaved a sigh. "I spent hours in the dark and you would have thought I'd be able to conquer the fear, but it only made it more intense. So much for being in charge of my life."

"Why do you need to be in control?"

"I'm a federal agent. Fear will hinder me."

"Perhaps, but I am here now. I will make certain that nothing happens to you."

"Men never stay." He had to strain his ears to hear her words. "That's why I need to take care of myself. When we are away from these guys, I'm taking you into headquarters."

"A Hunter's bond is never broken." Partlan's voice cracked. "I will do anything to protect you."

"Men leave as soon as they have what they want." Agent Kelly shifted her body. "I have the scars to prove it."

"They hurt you?" Partlan's chest tightened. "Where?"

"My scars are psychological, not physical." She cleared her throat. "My brother locked me in cupboards. My father left when I was seven and even though I begged him to take me, he refused."

Her voice faltered and for several minutes there was silence.

"In school, I fell in love with a football player. We made love and he promised me forever. Instead, the guy broadcast it to his teammates and they harassed me all through high school. I had to live with my shame until I was old enough to move away to college."

"They had no honor." His outrage filled the small space. "On my planet, they would have been killed for such actions."

"They were boys." Her tone was dismissive. "You would think I'd learn after all of those failures, but I still believed in true love and happily ever after. I even went so far as to get engaged."

"You were mated?"

"Almost. He ran out the day of the wedding and left me with all of the bills."

"So you do not believe a man can be honorable."

"I haven't met one who is." Her voice was derisive. "I'm a survivor and it made me tough. That's why I joined the FBI. I have a career and that's all I need. I take care of myself."

"I will never fail you."

"We'll see."

Agent Kelly's tone warned that it was impossible to change her mind. Partlan sensed the pain and degradation she had suffered at the hands of men and he wanted to take that from her. That was why he had been chosen to be pair bonded with her. She needed a man who lived with honor and understood commitment.

"I do have one question." Partlan's tone was tentative. "I have not known you for long, but would it be disrespectful to ask you what your name is? I cannot continue to call you Agent Kelly."

She chuckled beside him. It was a low rumble that set her body moving. "It's Grace. I don't want any jokes about that, though."

"What is funny about Grace? It is a beautiful name."

"Grace Kelly." Her tone was wry. "My father picked the name and I'm certain he did it for a joke."

"I do not understand."

"The actress who married a Prince?"

Partlan shook his head. "I am new here."

She moved up on her elbow. In the darkened space, she was no more than a shadow above him. "You honestly don't know?"

"No."

She moved back down on her side. "That's good." She snuggled close to him and within a few minutes her steady breathing let him know that she had fallen asleep.

Grace.

He repeated her name in his head. He like the way it sounded and how it fit with her looks and personality. She was the most gorgeous woman he had ever seen. Her light blonde hair and deep blue eyes were unknown on Cygnus. She was a creature of grace and beauty.

She understood how to command.

She was a true warrior.

His heart swelled with pride as he thought of how lucky he was to have found her. She was a worthy pair bond. There was only one problem. She did not have all the facts about the Albireons. They were not to be trusted. The fact that they were able to move freely among the people on Earth suggested that they had been here for a while. They were a species that the Kaladin had worked hard to exterminate from their territories. Centuries of fighting had finally achieved peace, and the disappearance of the Albireons. His people did not care where they had gone. They were just grateful to have harmony in their outer territories.

As a Hunter, that meant most of his time was spent in keeping peace nearer to home. Once he had joined Ardal's unit, he had been stationed on Cygnus itself. As the elite team of Hunters that protected the high council, he had no longer been sent across the territories to control outbreaks. His experiences with Albireons had happened on his first campaigns, but he remembered them.

They did not fight with honor.

They used deception and lies.

If they were on Earth, then this planet was at risk of being taken over by one of the most ruthless races in the universe. The resources of the world would be stripped. That was always the first step in their planned annihilation of a planet. Usually, the Albireons were able to convince a select few to agree to this strategy, with the understanding that there was a profit to be made. Then, when it was least expected, the indigenous species would be wiped out.

Albireons profited by gene harvesting.

When they had finished collecting genes from a species, they no longer needed them. Genetic recombination and gene splicing ensured that they could create new species that could be sold as slaves or workers to other planets. This is how the Albireons thrived. This is what made them a universal scourge. The Kaladin's had outlawed the selling of genomes, but since the civil revolution on his home planet of Cygnus, the Holman had made overtures to the Albireons.

It was only a matter of time before they were allowed back into Partlan's home galaxy.

He had to alert the other Hunters.

He sent out a mind connection to Ardal. *"I have left the hospital. Do not let any of the brothers near. Albireons are searching for me."*

Ardal answered. *"I'll alert the team I sent to rescue you. Find your way back to the nearest safe house. You must not be captured."*

"Understood."

It was better if the Albireons only knew about one Hunter being on the planet. He could not risk any of the others being found. He shifted in the small box and stretched his shoulders. Grace wanted to take him to the FBI headquarters because she thought that was safest. He would obey her, because he had promised. Afterwards, he would arrange for their safe conduct to the nearest Hunter team.

If she refused to listen to his advice, then he would have to convince her to come with him. As horrible as it was to think of disobeying a woman, he could not leave her to die at the hands of the Albireons. He would rather die himself than allow anything to happen to her.

Just then a loud bang sounded outside their container.

A door had slammed against the wall.

Grace jumped in his arms. "Someone is outside."

"It is best if we remain quiet." Partlan's voice was a low whisper.

Footsteps sounded near them.

The low murmur of voices came next.

Partlan eased his breathing and heartbeat. If the container was opened, he wanted to be prepared. He took Grace's gun and cocked and aimed it in readiness. He slid his other arm away from Grace and prepared himself to attack. He positioned his left leg so that it could propel his body upwards if necessary.

The footsteps stopped beside them.

Grace exhaled a soft breath that brushed across his cheek. His muscles tensed. There was a sharp jarring against the outside of the container. Partlan could feel the side of the box indent against him. It was a hand.

"Are these the ones slated to be moved to the Memories Funeral Home?" A stranger's voice boomed out.

"Best check them first."

Chapter 8

A shuffle of feet approached them.

Something pushed down on the lid.

Partlan aimed the gun so that he would be ready to shoot once the lid was opened. Grace's body tensed beside his and her fingers tightening on his shirt. Her breathing slowed and he knew she was readying herself for a battle also. Both of them were focused on preventing their capture.

"Looks like the right label." The voice was above them. "No need to look inside."

"Good. I hate dead bodies."

"You're in the wrong line of business then."

"It pays the bills." The depression on the top of the box disappeared. "Let's move them."

Partlan exhaled the breath he'd been holding. Grace released his shirt and sagged back against his side. There was a jolting of the box and then it was being rolled along the floor. The clanging of squeaky metal wheels against the tile was in stark contrast to the muted breathing inside the casket. They were jostled over a ramp and then pushed against a barrier with such force that they rocked back and forth before settling upright.

"We are in a vehicle." Partlan kept his voice low.

"On our way to the funeral home." Her words were tinted with sarcasm. "This is not how I wanted to go to a mortuary."

"Is there a good way to go there?" Partlan's tone was dry.

Grace choked back a laugh. "I think that's the first humorous thing I've heard you say."

"There has been little reason for levity."

"And you think on our way to a cemetery in a box reserved for the dead, is the right time?"

"It has made you forget our predicament."

"I suppose." Grace sighed. "I wish I had another phone."

"It is too easy to track us."

"What's the plan once we've been dropped off?"

"My orders are to find the nearest team." Partlan kept his tone neutral. "I have warned away any reinforcements because of the Albireons."

"Is your team close to the FBI headquarters?"

"No."

"Then it's a no-go. You said that you would follow me to headquarters. I think the FBI is the safest way to protect you. After that, we can see what happens. What I need to know is if you've considered what we do when this vehicle stops?"

Partlan fought back his objection. Every instinct in him knew that going to the Federal Headquarters was wrong. It was dangerous. They already knew that he had been detained by the FBI and they would be certain to watch the building. He had given his word, and he would not disappoint her. As long as there was no immediate threat at her office, then he would lead her there.

"As you wish." Partlan touched her arm. "If there is any risk, I will not take you there. My job is to protect you and that is what I mean to do."

"I can defend myself." Grace cleared her throat. "Which reminds me. You still have my gun. I'll need it back."

"You do not understand the menace you are up against."

"You mean the Albireons?" Grace's voice was severe. "If they are truly extraterrestrials, like you claim, then I'll deal with that as I would any other criminal. I'll arrest them. I refuse to announce to the office that we're being chased by ET."

"They cannot help us if you do not let them know what the threat is."

"They'll lock both of us up in the looney bin." Grace shifted her body so that her face was closer to him. "You may want to use that as your defense, but I will not have my career ruined over this. You're my responsibility and I'm taking you into headquarters where you'll be safe."

"You do not need to be upset." Partlan kept his voice low. "When we are outside, I will return your weapon. I have agreed to do as you ask."

"Good." Grace crossed her arms. "Bakker said that it was safe, so that's where we're going."

A door slammed and the vehicle jerked forward before the motion of the truck eased them away from the hospital. The sounds of traffic could be heard. Partlan held his breath as he counted the seconds until he could be certain they were free of the Albireons' reach. As long as no one checked what vehicles had left the hospital's loading dock, they should be safe.

About twenty minutes later the vehicle stopped. The back door of the truck was rolled up and he could hear the mumbled complaints of their drivers. He tightened his grip on the pistol and readied himself for a fight, but it wasn't necessary. They were moved off the vehicle, down an elevator, and rolled to a stop, without anyone looking inside. He released his breath and waited until no voices could be heard. He shifted in the container and tried to ease his body upright.

"Ready?"

"My body feels like a pretzel." Grace groaned. "I need to move."

Partlan stretched his neck and then lifted the lid an inch. His eyes scanned the room. There was no one in sight. He pushed back the plastic top of the box and sat up with the gun ready as he completed his search of the room. They were alone. He heaved himself out of the box and put his hand out for Grace.

She took it and climbed out of the coffin. Her feet wobbled and she was bent at the waist for a couple of seconds. She inhaled a couple of deep breaths before straightening her body. She rolled her shoulders and planted her hands on her hips and stretched her body up and backwards.

Partlan's breath caught in his throat.

A jolt of desire hit him.

Never had he looked at a woman and felt a need to gather her close and kiss her. His heart beat fast and an ache twisted his stomach. He longed to hold her. His whole body was on alert and there was only one thing that he craved.

Grace.

He clenched his jaw and forced his eyes away. Danger surrounded them and his focus had to be on protecting Grace. The legends were right. The lure of one's pair bond was distracting and exhilarating at the same time. He understood why a mate was forbidden to Hunters. He was a warrior, and nothing would prevent him from defending Grace.

His eyes roamed the room. It looked to be a laboratory of sorts. There were a couple of steel tables and with tubing connected to a machine. There were also trays with forceps, needles, and what looked like cakes of powder and brushes. It was a strange combination of instruments.

"What is this place?"

Grace went over to one of the tables and picked up a small clamp. "It looks like we're in the room where they do the embalming. We should be thankful they didn't send us straight to the crematorium."

"Explain."

"We're in a funeral home." Grace looked at him with an expectant look.

"I know." He shook his head. "This is where you take the dead, but what do you do with them?"

Grace moved away from the table filled with steel instruments. "We either cremate the dead, which means we burn the bodies, or we bury them. If they are to be buried, the body is preserved and this is where they do it."

"Understood." Partlan nodded. "On Cygnus, there is no space for burying our dead."

"So they're cremated."

"Unless we are in space. Then, the body is jettisoned out of the ship."

Grace tilted her head. "If I believed in aliens that would make sense."

"I do not lie."

"I know." Grace glanced around the room and then let out a small shriek. "Why didn't you tell me my hair was a mess?"

"I do not see a problem."

She walked over to a small mirror on the back of a white cupboard. "I look like I have a rat's nest on my head."

She shook her hair out of the bun and then yanked her fingers through it. Sparks of static sizzled from her blonde locks. She was ruthless in dealing with the flyaway hair and within seconds, she had it tamed, and clipped back into a neat bun at the back of her head.

Partlan was fascinated by her efforts. Women did not pull their hair off their faces on Cygnus. If their hair was long, it was meant to be shown, not kept hidden in a bun. Human women did many things different from those on his home planet, but this was the first time he had ever observed a woman this closely. Now, he wanted to know everything about Grace.

"I need my gun back." Grace held out her hand.

"As you wish." Partlan handed the weapon to her. He would have preferred to be armed, but he was proficient in hand to hand combat, and could easily defend Grace if necessary.

"Let's go." She holstered her weapon. "The longer we wait, the better chance we'll run into someone coming to embalm the new arrivals."

Partlan went to the door and glanced through the window at the top. The hallway outside was empty. He motioned Grace to stay behind him. They made their way down the hall and to another door. It led to a short rise of stairs that opened up into a formal area with several rooms leading off it. There was plush beige carpeting and numerous chairs spread around. Low murmurs were coming from down the hall, but that was the only indication that others were in the building. A glimmer of sunlight came through a door.

They headed outside.

They exited from a side entrance. They were momentarily blinded by sunlight, but after a few seconds their eyes adjusted. There were manicured lawns and gardens all around them. A lush oasis in the middle of the bustle and noise of the city. The sound of traffic and the smell of exhaust filled the air despite the illusion of peace. They walked across grass, around small ponds, and headstones until they found themselves on a side street.

Cars and trucks were everywhere; horns were honking, tires screeching, and people yelling. It was a relief after the hushed silence of the funeral home. Partlan's nose twitched at the smell of car fumes and tilted his head up at the street lights to see if any cameras were directed at the sidewalk. Everything seemed to be pointed at the main street and not along the side streets. It looked safe.

"We need to move."

"You look out of place with that hospital gown." Grace grabbed his arm. "There's a small strip mall down the street. There has to be a store in there that sells souvenir tee shirts. Anything would look better than what you have on now."

They walked toward the store at a brisk pace. Partlan surveyed the area and the people as they approached the row of stores. Nothing looked out of place. He refused to relax his vigilance until they were safe. Grace seemed to think her office was that place. Experience had taught him that it was the worst possible place for them.

The store offered a limited variety of shirts. Grace picked through a rack of them, pulling out and rejecting at least ten before she decided on one. It had a giant red heart on it, with the words I and Hollywood before and after. He was certain he had seen others wearing similar shirts, so he should blend in. She held it up to his chest and stood back to assess it. Her nose scrunched up a bit before she sighed.

"It'll have to do." She took it to the cash register. "It'll be small on you, but there's nothing in a larger size."

When she'd paid for it, she handed the shirt to him. "Put it on."

Partlan grinned. "You are well suited for the role of command."

She had been walking toward the door, but she turned to look at him with her eyes narrowed. "Is that a criticism?"

"No. It is admirable." Partlan took her arm and led her out of the store before he shrugged the shirt over his head. "On Cygnus, all women rule, but here on Earth I have found that very few are used to it."

Grace looked as if she were going to say something and then she shook her head and walked in the opposite direction of the funeral home. When they had gone several blocks, she stopped and looked at a bus sign.

"I don't think we should risk a taxi. The bus will be safer."

Partlan looked for cameras, but again everything seemed to be aimed at the road. It was a few minutes wait before a bus with the number four pulled up and stopped. They boarded and moved to the rear, where there were empty seats. One bus change, and an hour later, they were let off on a street near the Federal Building where Grace worked.

"Are you certain this is what you want to do?"

Partlan was getting an uneasy tightening in the pit of his stomach. His inner warning system was seldom wrong. Danger was near. Grace stopped walking and gnawed her lower lip. She looked at the building and then down the road.

"Bakker said it was safe, but I have a bad feeling about this."

"We should not go in there."

"Perhaps you're right." Grace's teeth continued to worry her bottom lip. "Let's keep walking until we find a phone. I'll call first."

They continued past the headquarters. They came up to a large building that housed several businesses and Grace climbed the stairs. It was all marble and granite flooring in the foyer and they walked past a central bank of elevators. Toward the rear of the building, there was one lone pay phone. Grace rummaged in her pocket and pulled out a few coins. After she dialed, she strummed her fingers on the edge of the large silver phone box until someone answered.

"Bakker it's me. Is it safe to come to the office?"

"Don't do it."

Partlan could hear the warning from where he stood. He leaned closer and Grace turned the phone so they both could listen.

"Those agency guys are everywhere." Bakker lowered his voice. "I don't know who they are, but I don't trust them. They want both of you now, not just Partlan. Carter has been holed up with them in his office for the last hour."

"That's not good."

"What on earth did you do to get these guys so angry?"

Grace glanced up at Partlan. "I wouldn't hand over my prisoner. Something wasn't right about the men who came for him."

"Well I'd lay low for a while, at least until things cool down."

Grace hung the phone up. "This was a wasted trip. I don't believe aliens are chasing us. That's a planned misinformation campaign by the government to keep military advances a secret."

"There is no time to argue. Let me take us to safety."

"We don't have much choice." Grace nodded. "Which way?"

They took a back exit out of the building and skirted along a few side roads. It was mostly residential low level apartment buildings. Partlan wanted to find a place to hide before he contacted his unit. That way they would be safe until rescue came for them.

There was rear parking behind one of the buildings. It was isolated. Redbud and dogwood trees provided shade and privacy. Partlan hesitated a second. There was a large brick wall at the end of the lot and no exit. They could not cut through the back of the buildings from there. There was a small laneway that ran along the next building. That would be a better route.

A black sports utility vehicle pulled up on the street beside them.

Four men jumped out of the car.

Partlan pushed Grace behind him and backed the two of them away. The men kept pace until they were directly in line with the parking lot. Partlan glanced both ways for an escape but another vehicle had pulled up and was blocking the sidewalk. The only choice was to stand and fight while Grace escaped in the opposite direction.

Grace had already pulled her gun out.

"Protect yourself." He motioned in the direction that was not blocked. "Do not let them catch you. Run."

Grace hesitated a second.

Partlan pushed her away.

"Leave." His voice softened. "It would be easier for me if I knew you were safe."

Grace glanced down the street where the men were approaching from. She nodded and then took off in the opposite direction. Partlan stretched his neck and clenched his fists as he prepared for battle. These men were armed with guns, but that did not matter.

Behind the men were two Albireons. They crossed their arms and then issued their orders.

"We want him alive."

Chapter 9

Grace stopped halfway up the street and looked back at Partlan. Her breath caught in her throat as she watched four men surround him. They were all dressed in black suits and had guns in their hands. She clenched her fingers around her pistol. It would be easy to go back and help, but she remembered the quiet confidence in Partlan's voice. He had been adamant in his request that she leave the area. She turned to run when an arm went around her neck from behind.

"Don't move."

She jerked her hand holding her weapon at him, but he grabbed her arm and pushed it down. "Drop it."

Grace tightened her grip on the gun. She wasn't going to be parted from her weapon. A squeeze around her throat had her gasping for air. He must have anticipated her escape and waited. It had been a trap, and like a fool, she'd walked right into his hands. She tried to turn around and face her attacker, but his hold was firm.

Her heart beat at a furious tattoo. "I'm an FBI agent. You're making a big mistake."

"Doesn't matter what you are. We're here to take you and the alien away. Now drop the weapon." His hand gripped her arm until she couldn't feel the circulation in her fingers. The gun fell to the ground.

He was as crazy as Partlan with his talk about aliens. "Are you working for his defense team?" Her tone was mocking as she struggled to twist her hand between her and her attacker's arm. He pulled her close and tightened his grip. "Quiet."

"I don't like being restrained." Grace flexed her numb fingers.

The man chuckled. "Get used to it. Where you're going there'll be no freedom until they decide you've served your purpose."

"I know my rights, and you're not only violating them, you're putting yourself at risk by holding a federal agent captive. You'll get life in jail."

"Your laws don't apply to me." The man squeezed her neck until the world blurred and started to spin.

She leaned into him and moved a leg back in an effort to loosen his grip, but his arm tightened. She twisted her body trying to break his hold. He pulled her free arm behind her back and yanked it up. Pain shot through her shoulder and made her gasp for air. She went limp.

She was out of choices.

She was caught.

Her captor dragged her back to where Partlan had already defeated two of his attackers. They were lying unconscious on the ground. The remaining two were aiming their guns at him. He kicked the weapon out of one attacker's hand and then twirled around and grabbed the second man's arm. He smashed the arm against his leg. Grace cringed at the sound of bones breaking.

Partlan brought the base of his hand up into the man's chin and sent him flying backwards. At the same time, Partlan's leg kicked the other opponent in the stomach. His adversary stumbled a couple of steps and then stood upright. By that time, Partlan had him in a choke hold and was about to break the man's neck when Grace's abductor yelled.

"Enough."

Grace was hauled over to Partlan. His eyes narrowed when he saw her. Anguish flickered in his eyes, and for an instant, a wave of regret and longing rushed through her. She must have imagined the look because the next second Partlan's face was impassive. His hands were still tight around his captive's neck.

"Let the woman go." Partlan's words were a threat. "You know I can destroy this man."

"Kill him" The man holding Grace inched her chin up a few inches. "He means nothing to me."

"You have no honor."

Grace's abductor chuckled. It rumbled deep in his chest and she felt the vibration through her body. Her stomach dropped at the true menace in his attitude. The man didn't care about anything but completing his mission. She'd met people like that before. Usually, it was when she'd had the misfortune to go up against national security agencies. They were true patriots who believed they had a righteous cause.

"You're so predictable, Hunter." The man's voice dropped to a low growl. "Surrender yourself or the woman dies."

"She has done nothing."

"She was caught with you. That is enough for the people I work with."

"It is me you want." Partlan threw his captive away from him. "Let her go."

"Down on your knees. Hands on your head." The commands were spit out in rapid fire. "I do not make deals with aliens."

"You will let the woman go."

"I'll kill her if you don't do as I say now." The man yanked up on her neck until she was standing on her toes.

Partlan looked at her and she thought she could hear his thoughts in her head. Be calm. I will protect you. She blinked and would have shaken her head if she could have moved it. She had to be hallucinating.

Partlan sank down onto his knees and put his hands behind his head. Before Grace registered that he was surrendering, one of their attackers came up behind Partlan and jabbed a needle into his neck. She opened her mouth to protest, but a cloth was shoved between her lips before she could say anything.

She watched Partlan sag lifelessly to the ground.

Bile rose in her throat and tears pricked her eyes.

For a second she thought they'd killed him, but one of the men kicked him over onto his back. She could see the steady rise of his chest and knew that he was breathing. Relief pulsed through her. It was crazy, but she was connected to Partlan.

"He's out." The man who kicked Partlan glanced up. "It'll take all of us to move him, though."

"You would never have captured him otherwise." The man holding Grace pushed her toward the SUV. "The one sure thing about a Hunter is that they will defend a woman to the death. They think it's an honor to die saving them."

"Now that shows a lack of smarts." The guy who'd injected Partlan shook his head. "What do we do with him now?"

One of the Albireons moved to Partlan. "Put him in the vehicle."

Grace wanted to scream at them to leave him alone, but the gag prevented any sound from escaping. She stomped her foot instead. Her reward was a tightening around her neck as she was hauled across the sidewalk to the SUV. She twisted her body, trying to attract the attention of someone on the street, but there was no one.

Three men lifted Partlan off the ground and carried him to the rear of the vehicle. They leaned his upper body against the open back and then lifted his legs up and pushed him inside. Grace was next. She was thrown in beside Partlan.

"No one can hear you scream except me and I promise that I will enjoy making you pay for each and every word you say." Her captor pulled the gag from her mouth.

"Who are you people?"

"Silence. I won't warn you again."

The back door was slammed shut. Grace scooted closer to Partlan. It was insane, but being near him gave her comfort. He was unconscious, unable to help her, yet knowing he was close, filled her with calm. She ran a quick hand over his body to check for any injuries. Despite taking on four large men, he was unhurt. If they hadn't threatened him with her death, he would have been able to escape.

Why had he tried to save her?

Her only thought throughout this whole ordeal had been to get him to headquarters. Her hand caressed his shoulder. He should be in a hospital bed recovering from the bullet wound that her team had inflicted on him. She cringed when she remembered the shooting. He had never once blamed her for his injuries. In the past, knowing that she'd been doing her job had always eased her doubts and guilt, but not this time.

Their captors settled into the vehicle and it pulled away from the curb. No one had tried to help them. It seemed impossible to believe that people could be abducted in broad daylight without someone noticing. What would the point be though? These men had clearance to do what they wanted and from what Bakker had said, they had thrown their weight around enough that even her position as a Federal agent didn't matter. Who did they work for?

Grace's mind darted from one possibility to the next. The law enforcement agencies might bicker over jurisdiction, but they wouldn't deliberately let another agent be taken. There was something very wrong about this group of men. They didn't fall under any organization that she was aware of. There was also the matter of the two Albireons who seemed to be in control. Were they aliens? Her stomach rolled with unease.

Her badge couldn't save them.

For the first time since they'd started running in the hospital, she questioned her ability to free them. These men didn't care about her position or the legalities of abducting a federal agent. They were either criminals, or a black ops division for some unknown defense unit. They certainly had the resources and men to do what they wanted.

She gave herself a mental shake. She was sounding like some conspiracy nut and that wasn't possible. Secret organizations and unsanctioned operations didn't happen in her world. She didn't believe in the existence of a shadow government that could run roughshod over people's rights. There had to be a logical explanation for what was happening to them.

She strained her neck to raise her head and look out the window of the car, but it was tinted so dark that it was impossible to see anything. They were locked into a small area at the rear of the vehicle. It had bars on the window and a dark glass barrier that separated them from the other occupants. It looked like something you'd keep an animal in.

She leaned back against Partlan and tried to stretch out the kinks in her legs. The men in the front of the vehicle were talking. She could hear murmurs of voices and she strained her ears to hear past the glass barrier, but it was no use. Until the vehicle stopped, there was nothing that she could do. She might as well get comfortable.

An hour later, the vehicle slowed and after a couple of turns, they stopped. Grace looked at Partlan's motionless body. Whatever they'd given him was very powerful. If she hadn't seen his chest rising and falling for herself, she would have thought he was dead. Her fingers trembled as she reached out to shake him awake. There was no response. A chill raced through her. What if he didn't wake up?

It made no sense, but she needed him to live.

Partlan mattered to her.

She had no use for men, but he had somehow worked his way into her heart. She wasn't sure when it had happened. Maybe when he'd tried to protect her from those strange visitors in his hospital room, or when he'd accepted her fear of the dark and helped her through it. All she knew was that when he'd knelt down and offered himself in place of her, he was no longer just her prisoner.

She trusted Partlan.

She was a woman who'd learned the hard way that she could only rely on herself. An abusive brother and being jilted at the altar had her swearing off men forever. It was different with Partlan. There was a bond that connected them. Partlan had tried to exchange his life for her freedom. Now it was her turn to fight.

She wouldn't let Partlan die.

She tensed her muscles at the slamming of the vehicle's doors. This would be her only opportunity to escape and she intended to be ready this time. Years of self-defense training would not be wasted. They might be bigger than her, but she had a black belt in martial arts.

The hatch was flung open. A blaze of sunlight blinded her. Before her eyes adjusted, she was being pulled from the vehicle. She leaned into her assailant and used his weight to throw him over her shoulder. She turned to grab his weapon when two men tackled her to the pavement. The click of the hammer of a gun sounded near her ear.

"You're expendable. There's nothing I'd like more than to dispose of you right now." The voice of the man who had originally grabbed her was deadly calm. "Our orders are to bring the Hunter back alive. There was nothing about you."

Grace stilled her breathing and looked up at the man. He was dark haired with emotionless steel grey eyes. "Then kill me."

There was several seconds of silence before the man removed his gun from the side of her head. "No. We can use you to control the Hunter."

The man straightened up. "Put her on the plane."

Chapter 10

A throbbing, searing ache filled his head.

He tried to connect with Ardal. Fog and a buzzing in his ears were the only response he received. He was alone.

Partlan moaned and stretched the cramps out of his legs. He was lying on a hard cement surface and damp was wicking up into his body. A shiver convulsed him. At the back of his brain was the flickering of a memory.

Grace.

A jab of terror ripped through him. He bolted upright and struggled to stand, but his legs gave beneath him. He shook his head and tried again. This time, he realized his arms were pinned behind his back. He clenched his jaw, focusing on a concrete wall beside him as he twisted his body to get free.

"There's no point in struggling." Grace's words echoed in the stone chamber. "I've tried everything and these cuffs are meant to hold."

She was alive.

His stomach tightened and his mouth went dry. For a second his heart stopped and then started pounding at a furious rate. He was not certain if it was a side effect of the drug given him or just the relief and joy of hearing her beloved voice.

He turned to look at her. She was sitting a few feet away, her back against the gray wall of their prison. Partlan's eyes widened at the change in her appearance. Her hair had fallen out of the bun that she usually wore, one side of her cheek was puffed out, and a bruise was forming near her eye. Her jacket was torn and her knees were exposed through her pants. Someone had hurt her.

Every muscle in his body tensed as he fought to contain his anger.

"Who did this to you?" His words came through gritted teeth.

"The guys who took us in Los Angeles." Grace sighed. "They injected you with something that put you out. You've been unconscious for hours."

"Where are we?"

"I have no idea. We were shoved on a plane and put in a dark holding cell. The plane was flying at least six hours before it landed, so we could be anywhere."

"They said they would let you go."

"They only wanted you to stop fighting." Grace pursed her lips. "I don't know who those guys are that took us, but they aren't working for any government agency that I know."

"They have no honor."

"I warned you about men." Grace's voice was dry. "I tried to escape and that's when I got roughed up."

"They have broken the Sacred Code. They hurt a woman and the punishment is death. They will die."

"Be my guest." Grace stretched her legs. "If I get to them first, I'll kill them myself."

"How long have I been out?"

"I can't be certain about the time." Grace shrugged. "I fell asleep, so I'd guess a day has passed since we were caught."

Partlan glanced up at the ceiling of their prison. It looked to be solid concrete, as did the walls. There was only one way into the cell and that was by a door with a small window. The window had a sliding closure that was shut now. He frowned as he examined all the corners of the room. There were no cracks or obvious places to hide a camera. There was a bare lightbulb in the center of the ceiling and it had no other wires or equipment attached to it. That meant there was no surveillance. They must think their prison was secure.

Fools.

He twisted his wrists back and forth. The cuffs that were holding him were tight, but the continued action of his wrists was weakening the metal of the restraints. He had to break these cuffs and get to Grace. His need was soul deep. She was in pain and he had to be certain that she was not hurt. By Cygnus and Warrior, if they'd laid a hand on her other than the bruises he saw, he would rip this place apart.

Power and determination surged through him.

The cuffs bent open and he freed himself from his chains.

Grace's eyes widened. "How did you do that?"

"This planet gives me many advantages." Partlan knelt next to her and brushed a hand over her discolored cheek. "Did they hurt you in any other way?"

Grace shook her head. "I fell when I tried to escape. That's why the bruises. I really don't think these guys care about anything other than their mission. They weren't interested in me as a woman."

Relief eased his tense muscles. "That is good. Let me get those cuffs off you."

"Look through my coat pockets. You might find something there."

"They are sloppy if they left you with a means of escape."

"Most men don't notice what women are carrying. All they cared about was my gun."

Partlan rifled through the front pocket of her suit jacket. He found a bobby pin. It would be easier to turn the lock than to rip it from Grace's wrist. He had the cuffs off within a minute, then he gathered her close. His heart pounded and he swallowed back his anguish as he took a steadying breath and tucked her head under his chin.

"You are certain you are not in pain."

Grace tried to push away, but he kept his arms around her. He should let her loose, but he needed her near. His whole being was tormented at how close he had come to losing her. Even if she had ordered him to release her, he doubted he would be able to obey. The tension eased from her and then she settle into his arms.

"My pride is hurt more than anything else." Her words were mumbled into his chest. "All my years of self-defense training and martial arts, and I couldn't escape those guys."

"There were too many of them." Partlan's breathing slowed as he heard the calm in her voice. She was truly unharmed. "Now we must find a way to leave this place."

"Good luck with that." Grace moved back and stared into his eyes. "We were locked in a small box and it was dark, but I counted at least seven floor indicator bells."

"So no one can hear us through these walls. It is the perfect prison. No wonder they are lax in the small details."

Partlan stood and ran his fingers over the walls and corners of the room. He moved higher to the ceiling and then examined the floor. There were no hidden devices. The room was solid cement block and there were no windows or mirrors on the walls. The door's sliding window was the only way to check the area without opening the door.

"We are not being watched."

Grace stood and arched her back in a stretch. "There are probably cameras outside. If it were possible to escape, then they would know when we left the cell."

"A Hunter is not easy to keep contained." Partlan walked back to Grace. "I have vowed to protect you. I will find a way to get us out of this place."

Their gazes locked and Partlan watched as a shadow of emotion flared and then disappeared in Grace's eyes. She was still hesitant to believe him. She had spent most of her life defending herself, but now she had him. In time, she would understand that a Hunter never broke his word.

Grace looked away. She shook each leg and then started to pace in their small cell. "Why do you think they've kidnapped us?"

"The Albireons must have great control of this planet to be able to move around freely." Partlan pushed away his unease. Albireons had been defeated before. "I suspect they have made some deal with the powers that rule your planet."

Grace put up her hand. "Stop right there. I'm not certain I can accept this talk of aliens and visitors from other planets. If that were really the case, why haven't we seen these extraterrestrials?"

"You are forgetting that I am not from your planet."

"You talk about your Sacred Code and being a Hunter, but you look exactly like a human." Grace ran her eyes over him. "You're taller and definitely more muscular, but essentially, you're physically the same as any other man."

"Even though we were born and bred on Cygnus, we were originally from this planet."

"Well that's a handy explanation." Grace raised an eyebrow. "You're human, but you come from a different planet."

"The Ancients have existed since the beginning of time. Until a few days ago, I thought that Hunters had been created by the Ancients to be protectors. My leader, Ardal, has learned that we have the same genes as humans."

"That proves that you're not an alien." Grace leaned against the stone wall with her arms crossed over her chest.

"We have been altered."

She frowned. "In what way?"

"We have special abilities that have been genetically enhanced. Hunters have been trained since birth to fight. We also have abilities that have been bred into us. Each of our clans has skills that are unique to them."

"What's your skill?"

"I am clan Obair. I have a gift for working with instruments and machines."

"You're an engineer."

"That is what you call it on your planet." Partlan rubbed his shoulder where the bullet had entered. His wound was only a slight ache, but lying with his hands behind his back had not helped it. Grace straightened away from the wall and came to him.

"Take your shirt off and let me look at it. It was too soon for you to be out of the hospital. Fighting with those agents must have aggravated the incision."

Partlan pulled the shirt over his head. Grace peeled back the edges of his dressing and then stopped.

"Is there a problem?"

"It's healed." Grace finished taking the dressing off and then moved him under the light in the center of the room. "That's impossible."

Partlan gazed down at her and marveled at her beauty and courage. He was connected to Grace. Her feelings were his, which only proved that she was his mate. There was no question about the bond between them. That's why her doubts were so clear to him. She did not believe him.

Somehow, he must make her understand their connection. Words were meaningless to her, so he could only show her by his actions and thoughts. He would do whatever it took to convince her that they were meant to be together. She was a reasonable woman and would eventually realize that they were pair bonded.

"This planet has given us many strengths. One of those is that we heal quickly."

"What are your other strengths?" Grace's voice was a whisper.

"We move faster, our reflexes are better and we age slower."

"How old are you?"

"I have seen thirty-three years since I was bred."

Grace tilted her head as her eyes roamed over his face. Partlan held his breath and remained as still as possible. He sensed that she was on the verge of accepting his origins. Her eyes left his face and then scanned his chest. Her fingers brushed over several of his scars. His stomach tensed. Her hand rested on his upper left arm.

"Where did you get these tattoos?"

"They are my markers."

She frowned. "What do they mark?"

"My birth, my clan and my battles."

Her fingers grazed over the black glyphs that were the symbols of the Kaladin language. She tapped one of them. "What is this?"

"It is the date of the Denebrics Campaign. We were successful and freed many Kaladin that had been taken captive on the outpost."

Grace bit her lower lip. "How did you get to Earth?"

"We crashed here almost a year ago." Partlan kept his voice calm. "We were being transported for execution and Ardal, our leader, chose to let us die with honor. We fought the extinction order and took over the spacecraft."

"Extinction order?" Grace's voice was hesitant. "Does that mean what I think?"

"All Hunters were order executed. There was a civil war on our planet and the Kaladin lost. The Holman took over and feared that Hunters would not obey them, so we were deemed obsolete. All breeding facilities on Cygnus were demolished. Our genomes were destroyed and any existing Hunters were terminated."

"Genocide is what we call it on Earth." Grace shivered. "How can you speak of it so calmly?"

"We were bred and trained for one purpose. We serve by protecting and fighting. To die with honor is the best we can hope for."

"You make it sound as if you were machines." Grace's fingers fluttered against his arm. "I've seen you injured. You're flesh and blood like any other human."

"We were bred to obey the Kaladin. We do not question our orders. That is why the Holman thought that we would go willingly to our death."

Grace nodded. "I'm assuming other Hunters fought too."

"No. All others obeyed the extinction order." Partlan put his shirt back on. "We were the last to be executed because we were away on a mission when the orders were given."

"So you are the only Hunters left?" Grace's voice sounded hollow.

Partlan nodded. "Less than half our unit survived the crash."

"That explains why those guys who kidnapped us are so eager to get their hands on you." Grace paced the small cell. "If you are human, but have modifications, then that means they want to understand what those changes are."

"Perhaps." Partlan rubbed the back of his neck. "They may also want us for our fighting ability."

"If they have your genes, they'll make more of you." Grace's voice was dry. "No, I think they need you for experimentation. If that is what they intend, then there is no need for me. I'm just here to make certain that you don't fight them. They have no intention of keeping either one of us alive."

"Escape is imperative." Partlan's tone was decisive. Grace finally understood the danger that they were in. She would not fight his protection of her.

There was a shuffling noise outside their cell. Partlan moved to the side of the door and crouched. He steadied his breathing and slowed his heart rate. His course was clear. He would kill the person who came through that door and fight for their freedom. He could not let Grace stay in this place and die.

There was a scraping sound and then the unbolting of a lock.

The door opened a crack.

Before Partlan could attack, a voice sounded in his head. "*I am Eogan, clan Rioge. Are you a Hunter?*"

Chapter 11

Grace's mouth dropped open at the size of the man who came through the entry. Partlan had been set to attack, but for some reason he stood and stepped away from the door. The newcomer had the same dark hair and eyes as Partlan. He slipped through a tiny opening of the door and closed it with an almost silent click. He glanced at her before his eyes dropped to the ground and he turned to Partlan.

"Hunter?"

Partlan nodded. "I am Partlan, clan Obair. Team leader, under the command of Ardal, protector of the High Council."

The stranger nodded. "Impressive."

Partlan took a step toward her. "Grace Kelly, this is Eogan. He is also a Hunter. Grace and I were kidnapped in Los Angeles several hours ago. Can you tell us where we are?"

"You are at a secret facility in Australia." Eogan's voice was clipped.

"No." It felt as if a hammer hit her in the chest and knocked the breath from her. How had they gotten all the way to Australia? "Why?"

"This facility monitors communications world-wide." Eogan leaned against the door. "I believe someone mentioned Hunter on a newscast and they sent scouts to see if it were true."

Grace winced. "The Walters. They complained to the media about how the FBI had treated Partlan."

"What did they do?" Eogan's tone was serious.

"We shot him."

Eogan nodded and turned to Partlan. "Have you recovered?"

"There is an ache, but the wound has closed."

"Good. If you're going to escape, then you must be fit." Eogan glanced at the ceiling. "Are there cameras?"

"I can find none."

Eogan walked away from the door. "There is one outside of your cell and I moved it so that if you stay close to the wall you can avoid being seen."

"How long have you been here?" Partlan crossed his arms. "We have not heard of a Hunter working alone on this planet."

"I have been at this place for several years, working for the different agencies that have been in charge. In recent years, the mission of the facility has changed. It is located so that no one may spy on it. There are secret areas that only a select few know about. You are in one of those areas." Eogan's eyes narrowed. "Understand, I do not do this by choice. I was taken when I was a child and my training and implants were tampered with. I am at the command of the humans."

"Did you crash land with Catal?" Partlan stepped closer to her.

"You know Catal?"

"He is now part of Ardal's unit. He has completed his training and is no longer a mercenary on this planet."

Grace raised a hand. They were talking about things she didn't understand. It all sounded very military though. It also seemed to confirm Partlan's story about being from another planet. "I thought you were all guns for hire."

"We are warriors who follow our own code, not the rules of humans." Partlan glanced at her and then motioned for her to come near.

He wasn't making sense, but nothing was. She took the couple of steps needed to be beside him. He gripped her arm and pushed her behind him. When she tried to step away, his grasp strengthened. She was getting tired of his caveman tactics. She was a trained federal agent. She could take care of herself.

"I won't hurt the woman." Eogan's words echoed in the cell. "I may have been forced to work for the humans, but I have not forgotten the Sacred Code. Women and children are to be protected always."

"How can I know that they haven't sent you in here as a trick?" Partlan eased his hold on her arm.

"The word of a brother and the vow of a fellow Hunter." Eogan sounded sincere.

Partlan hesitated a second and then released her arm. She rubbed the area where his hand had been as she came out from behind him. The two men were glaring at each other, until Partlan nodded and relaxed.

"I will trust you."

"I mean no harm." Eogan took a step closer. "You are the first contact I've had in over thirty years. The silence has been painful."

"I cannot imagine." Partlan cleared his throat. "Why can I not reach my unit?"

"There is an energy field that makes this place invisible to communication listening devices. It also makes it impossible to connect to someone outside. You are the first Hunter I have sensed since I was brought here."

Grace shook her head. They were talking in riddles, and all she wanted to know was what the escape plan was.

"How soon can we leave this place?"

Eogan looked at her. "I will have to arrange the escape. You are down seven levels and it will be noticed if you leave."

She had been right about the number of floors they had passed. Never had she thought those floors were below ground. Her heart stuttered and panic clouded her brain. For the first time she let herself think about what that meant. It was dark below ground. The walls could cave in and they'd be buried alive. Her breathing came in gasps. Her knees weakened, forcing her to sit on the ground. Partlan knelt beside her.

"Breath." His voice held concern.

She shook her head. Words jumbled in her mind, but nothing came out. Out of nowhere, the sensation of peace came over her. The knot in her chest loosened and she forced out a breath. Partlan's hand rubbed her back and she leaned into the comfort he gave. Her next breath was easier.

"I will not leave you. There is no need to be afraid."

"What's the problem?" Eogan was beside them now.

"She fears the dark and small places."

"Claustrophobia. Make her stand and walk." Eogan's tone was authoritative.

Partlan helped her up and then held her close, as they walked back and forth in the room. The tension in her body eased and her heart rate returned to normal.

"I feel like an idiot." Grace could have kicked herself for her reaction.

"It's normal for newcomers to this facility to experience what you did." Eogan lifted her face to his and frowned. "Your eyes have not returned to normal, but your breathing is better."

"Is it being below ground that affects people?" Grace straightened away from Partlan.

"Probably, but it's safe. Everything has been reinforced. There's no way signals can penetrate to this level, so we can use that to plan your escape."

"Don't we need to contact someone to help us?" Grace couldn't envision how they would manage to get to the surface without assistance.

"It's a dead zone, with arrays of blocking frequencies surrounding it. Nothing comes in, or goes out, unless it's designed to." Eogan crossed his arms over his massive chest. "Between Partlan and myself, we'll be able to coordinate a plan."

Grace's eyes narrowed. There was something that Partlan wasn't telling her, but her brain refused to deal with it. If they had a secret way for them to get out of this hellhole, then she wasn't going to spoil it with questions. All she wanted was to go home and have a long soak in her own bathtub. If she could, she would have turned the clock back four days, and let Partlan walk away after he'd delivered the Walters' boy to his parents. Then, all of this would disappear, like a bad dream.

"How were you able to get to us?"

"They no longer believe I will disobey them." Eogan's eyes were distant. "Until I sensed you near, I had no reason to. I thought I was alone on this planet."

"We are brothers and fight together. You will escape with us and we will find our way back to the unit." Partlan clenched his hands into fists. "The humans have done you a great dishonor."

"I'm not leaving." Eogan shook his head. "I have only just discovered the existence of more Hunters. It's too soon for me to make a decision. Besides, if we both escape they will track me and that will endanger you."

"You will follow us after we have gone." Partlan's words were a statement. "It is necessary for you to know what has happened to the rest of our brothers."

Eogan frowned. "Have you found a way off this planet?"

"There is no home for us. All Hunters were ordered executed."

"Why?"

"There was a civil war on Cygnus and the Kaladin were defeated by the Holman. It was feared that Hunters would only obey the Kaladin so we were ordered terminated." Partlan's voice was emotionless. "We were luckier than the other Hunters. Our leader,

Ardal, chose to allow us to die fighting. We disobeyed the execution order and fought for control of the ship carrying us to our death. That is when we crashed on this planet."

Eogan cleared his throat. "How many Hunters survived?"

"We number over one hundred." Partlan's voice held pride. "There are also those who crashed when you did. They are at least eighty strong and now form part of Ardal's unit. All of clan Rioge was exterminated. Ardal will be thankful one of his clan survives."

"For years, I thought I was the only Hunter on this planet. Now, I have much to hope for."

"There is even more. We are able to live a normal life. Much has happened since we have removed our implants." Partlan rubbed an area over his right forearm. "We have learned that many of our legends are true. Three of our unit have found pair bonds and are mated."

Eogan's eyes widened. "Is this true?"

"What's a pair bond?" When there was no answer, Grace pulled on Partlan's arm. "Explain this please."

Eogan was the one who spoke first. "Legend has it that a Hunter is destined to bond with one mate for life. They share a bond that cannot be broken even by death. That is why a Hunter is forbidden to mate. His bond is so strong that he will disobey orders to protect his mate. All else is forgotten, if a Hunter's mate is in need."

"Our implants had been deactivated when we were loaded onto the prison ship, so we were no longer receiving enhancements." Partlan's tone was quiet. "On earth, it was discovered that part of what the implant did was to ensure that we would not form a pair bond."

"You weren't allowed to marry?" Grace's voice rose with indignation. "What kind of people were these Kaladin?"

"We were bred to protect them. It was forbidden for a Hunter to mate."

"Ever?"

"A Hunter may not be with a woman." Eogan's voice was matter of fact. "It might distract him from his duty, which is to protect and follow orders."

"So you guys have never had a relationship with a woman?" She didn't bother to hide her disbelief.

"Never." Partlan's eyes locked onto hers.

There seemed to be a silent message that he was trying to convey. She inhaled and broke contact. For a second, she'd thought she'd heard his voice in her mind telling her that they were connected. That had to be her imagination. She'd never been a person who believed in anything telepathic or supernatural, and she wasn't going to start now. She was tired and stressed. That was the only explanation.

Partlan turned back to Eogan. "Have you never felt a connection with a woman?"

"No." Eogan shook his head. "My implants are still effective. When I was first captured, the enhancements that the Kaladin had put in place were tampered with. Once the humans understood what they were, they altered them to fit their needs."

"You must remove them."

"They have other ways to control us." Eogan's tone was dry. "There's a constant bombardment of electrical energy that affects behavior. I think it interferes with the connection between Hunters outside of this compound. Today was the first I had ever sensed another brother. I knew that meant you were within these walls. It was easy to find you."

"You cannot stay here." Partlan's tone was insistent. "They will know you helped us leave."

"I am useful to the humans. They trust me. I can come and go as I please within the compound. I'll be able to arrange your escape."

"There must be another way." Partlan lifted his chin. "I will not leave you here to face these monsters alone. We will attack the whole compound."

"It won't work." Eogan lowered his voice. "It's vast. It's a multi-national effort that is at a level higher than most heads of state. Some of this planet's oldest organizations and moneyed families signed a treaty with the Albireons when they first came to Earth over seventy years ago. In exchange for technological advances, they allowed the Albireons control."

"You cannot expect me to leave a brother behind?"

Grace bit her lower lip. Escape sounded as if it would be dangerous, even if they all went together. To attack the whole unit was asking for disaster. The odds were against them. They needed a different plan.

"They trust me." Eogan's tone was persuasive. "Until now, I didn't know that there were other Hunters on this planet. The humans kept me alive because I was clan Rioge. All of the others that were captured, have been killed."

"That means they intend to kill us too." Grace's heart skipped a beat.

"Yes." Eogan nodded. "They frequently send me on missions outside the compound. On my next mission, I will contact you. From there, I will make my escape."

"Are you certain they will not discover that you arranged our release?"

Eogan crossed his arms over his chest. "I am the last person they would suspect. They truly believe that I can't disobey an order. Their implants have kept me doing their bidding since, I was a child. It will be a relief to no longer obey."

Partlan hesitated a second before nodding. "If you do not contact us, we will come back to free you."

"That won't be necessary." Eogan opened the door. "I'll let you know when it is safe to leave."

A second later, Eogan was gone. Grace frowned. How was he going to let them know? They didn't have any cell phones.

"Is he going to come back here? That could be dangerous."

"He will not risk seeing us again."

"Then how will you know when to leave?"

"Eogan will use mind connection."

Grace tilted her head. The term sounded strange. "What's that?"

Partlan took her hands in his. "Hunters can connect without words."

"Like telepathy?"

"Something like that. We sense when one of us is near or in danger." Partlan hesitated a second and then continued. "The same connection is possible between pair bonds."

"The women you mate with."

Grace's voice was a whisper. Her heart was pounding and she had to force herself to breath. This connection he spoke of, sounded like love. That was a fairy tale, not reality. A bond like he was describing didn't exist. She had secretly longed for it since she had been a little girl. Life, and men, had forced her to forget her dreams of a forever love.

"We only mate with one woman. That woman is our pair bond. If she refuses us, then we will never mate with another."

"That's pretty drastic." Grace tried to pull her hands away from Partlan, but he held tight, his gaze never wavering from her. She swallowed the lump in her throat. "Why are you telling me this?"

"You need to understand that if we are separated, you can communicate with me."

"I'm not telepathic."

"I will hear you." Partlan leaned close. "We are connected. You are my pair bond."

Chapter 12

Grace pulled her hands away from Partlan. "I've sworn off men for the rest of my life."

"Nevertheless, we are bonded." Partlan's tone was quiet. "You were the reason I came back to Beverly Hills."

"I thought you wanted to bring the Walters' boy back."

"I could have sent him by himself. I knew he would be safe." Partlan's voice dipped low. "I needed to see you."

"We hardly spoke."

Grace fought back the surge of emotion that Partlan's words were causing. A vice grip was tightening its hold on her chest. She didn't want to be connected to a man, least of all one that was from another planet.

She couldn't deny that she was attracted to him.

Being near him, gave her joy.

She shook her head and turned away. It couldn't be possible. There was no way that she could be connected with a man who flaunted the law. She believed in the justice system and it was her job to ensure that it was obeyed. Partlan believed in his Sacred Code and he didn't care about breaking the law to protect his code.

"You still fear me." Partlan's voice held sadness. "I would never harm you."

"We are opposites," Grace whispered. "We would never agree on anything."

"You fight for what you believe is right, as do I." Partlan took a step toward her. "I protect those who need it. So do you. How are we different?"

"You kill people who don't agree with your code."

"Do you not do the same?" Partlan's eyebrow rose. "When I did not follow your rules, I was shot."

Grace's eyes widened. He was right. Had she really tried to detain him because he broke the law, or had it been because he challenged her authority? Was part of her determination to hold him because she feared how she reacted when he was near?

She couldn't deny that she longed to have his arms around her and to feel safe.

Partlan's eyes hadn't left her face. "I sense that you are uncertain. I will not force anything on you, but I will always be here if you need me."

"Men always leave."

"Not a Hunter." Partlan's voice was sincere. "We bond for life and even if you chose to mate with another, there will always be a connection. I could never leave you. Even in death, I will always be with you."

"How could you possibly promise that?" Grace shook her head.

"As our bond grows stronger, we will be able to share everything with each other, including our thoughts."

Grace bit her bottom lip. Partlan spoke with reverence of this bond, but she didn't know if she wanted to be connected with someone so closely. To have them aware of her every thought seemed invasive, and yet a small part of her was intrigued. To be linked with another person and know that you could rely on them would be less lonely. It would ease the tension and stress of having only yourself to rely on.

She pushed the thought away.

Survival meant trusting no one.

Grace lifted her chin. "I need to be strong and protect myself."

"The bond will not interfere with that." Partlan gave a slight bow of his head. "Remember that I am here always. All you have to do, is reach out to me with your mind. You may not want my protection, but I cannot let any harm come to you. Even if we are never together as mates, I am destined to be your protector."

Grace rubbed her temple. It was too much to consider all at once. "It's difficult to believe everything you've told me."

Partlan gathered her close, rubbing a soothing hand down her back. A wave of calm ebbed through her. There was no other place she wanted to be. It didn't matter that they were being held prisoners in a concrete cell, or that the people holding them would kill them. All she cared about was being close to Partlan. She had to be crazy.

"It is easier not to fight the attraction." His voice was a throaty whisper. "The bond is real. I fought it myself in the beginning because I did not believe. I was helpless against the strength of the connection. I had to be with you, even when it meant my own capture."

Grace leaned into Partlan and closed her eyes. She let the peace and protection he offered flow through her. An urgent craving to know what it would be like to kiss him, overwhelmed her. She gazed up at him as wisps of desire curled inside her. Partlan seemed to understand. He bent and brushed his lips over hers.

Fire and passion rushed through her.

Her lips clung to his, as need overcame fear.

She sighed, luxuriating in the shivers of heat that danced through her. Delicious tendrils of pleasure coiled deep in her womb. She was lost in the touch and feel of Partlan. Her tongue darted into his mouth and twirled around his. Shards of delight sparked and lit flames of excitement that radiated from her inner core.

She yearned for more.

Her hands roamed up his firm chest, reveling in the thrill of bliss that settled within her. Partlan was perfect in every way. A shudder of exquisite joy caressed every part of her before the kiss ended. Their breathing was ragged as they rested their foreheads together.

"That was insane." Grace inhaled a shaky breath.

"I have never felt anything like that." Partlan's voice shook. "There can be no doubt we are bonded."

Grace took a step back. She needed time to consider everything that had happened. Partlan was insisting that they were meant to be together and a part of her wanted that to be true. Past relationships had shown her that there were no happy endings. She had never experienced anything as spectacular as that kiss, though.

"I need time to think." Grace ran a shaky hand through her hair. "I don't do well with relationships. Men always leave."

"I am not like other men."

Grace blew a strand of hair out of her eyes. "No, you're not, but I am still the same woman."

Before she could say anything else, there was the sound of footsteps outside of their cell. Partlan motioned for her to go back to the corner where she'd been cuffed. He did the same thing. Her heart pounded in her ears as she held her breath. Now they would find out why they'd been taken and how soon they could leave.

There was a rattle of the handle and then the steel door swung open. The man who'd taken them in Beverly Hills walked into the cell and looked first at Partlan and then at her. He had two armed men in uniform behind him and he motioned for them to enter. Grace didn't recognize the uniform insignias, but their stance proclaimed them as military. They looked like they would obey orders and shoot on demand.

"Isn't this cozy." The man's grey eyes narrowed as he glanced between Grace and Partlan.

"Who are you?" Grace forced her voice to remain calm.

"You can call me Ian, but I doubt we'll know each other long enough to be on a first name basis."

"Abducting a federal agent carries a long prison term." Grace lifted her chin. "My office will be looking for me."

"Right now, your supervisor is being advised that you were killed when your prisoner attempted to escape." Ian sounded bored. "This is not the first time we have had to remove law officers who have interfered."

"I did no such thing." Indignation rose in her chest. "I was protecting my prisoner. You were the ones who insisted on kidnapping him."

"Your case means nothing to us." Ian's eyes narrowed. "You have no idea what you're involved in."

"Enlighten me."

"We are a global conglomerate. We don't answer to governments and definitely not to their law enforcement agents."

"You need money to run that kind of a business."

Grace's throat went dry. A world-wide covert operation such as he described made her mind spin. How could such a group exist and the rest of the world not be aware of it? Better yet, why would any government not know that Ian's people were working within their borders? They must be sanctioned by someone and that suggested a conspiracy of monstrous proportions.

"Money is of no consequence." Ian shook his head. "You still don't get it. The people I work for, run the world, not just one country. We answer to no one. We make people like you disappear on a daily basis."

"You won't get away with it."

"Watch me." Ian motioned to the men behind him. "Take the woman."

"No." Partlan's voice boomed.

Ian's upper lip rose in a sneer. "You're in no position to dictate."

"She stays, or you will regret it." Partlan stood away from the wall and flexed his hands into fists.

"I see you broke your restraints." Ian shrugged. "Do it again and the woman dies."

Partlan's eyes narrowed. "You would dishonor a woman?"

"I do whatever it takes to get what I need." Ian took a step closer to Partlan. "Right now, we want information from you. The woman has only one use."

"Your words have sealed your fate." A muscle tightened in Partlan's jaw.

He threw a pair of cuffs at Partlan. "Put these on one of your wrists or I'll kill the woman right now." He aimed and cocked a pistol at Grace.

Partlan picked up the cuffs and put them on his wrist. "These will not stop me."

"Knowing I will harm her, will stop you from fighting us." Ian motioned Partlan to move toward the wall. "Put the other half on the metal ring in the wall."

Partlan glared at him for a second and then looked at Grace. He snapped the cuff to the ring and then stood away from the wall as far as his restraints would hold. "Let her go."

"She leaves when I say."

The two uniformed men moved toward her. Grace backed against the wall and when they reached for her, she twisted out of their reach. When she would have dodged their hands again, Ian yelled.

"Enough." His voice was like the crack of a whip. "You go with them or I will kill the Hunter in a long and torturous series of knife cuts. There will be nothing left of him because I will fillet every inch of skin from his body until he begs for death."

"A Hunter does not beg." Partlan's tone was scornful.

Grace's arm was grabbed by one of the men and she was dragged to the open door. A wave of panic hit her. She was going to be separated from Partlan. Her eyes widened as she looked at him. It hit her with blinding clarity that she never wanted to be away from him. She needed him with her always. He was as essential as breathing.

"I will find you."

Partlan's words were a vow. His eyes never left her face as she was dragged out of the room. For a fleeting second, she thought she heard his voice in her head telling her to believe in their connection.

Grace struggled to escape, but her captor's grip was too strong. Her arm was twisted behind her back and she was dragged down a long concrete hallway. There were spotlights on the ceilings at twenty foot intervals, but shadows still clung to the edges of the walls. She shivered as the thought of what might lurk in their dark depths, played at the edge of her imagination.

She took a deep calming breath.

She'd survived worse.

Her nightmares, when she was a child, had been a figment of her imagination. This was real. She forced the thought away. She needed to stay focused. She counted the steps they were taking and the directions they took, to commit them to memory. When she escaped she would be able to find her way back to Partlan.

She was pulled to a stop in front of a brushed steel elevator door. It had Level 7 written on its door. When it opened, she was thrown against the back wall and one of her captors pushed up against her. For a second, she thought he was going to attack her, but all he did was glare at her, daring her to move.

The doors shut and the elevator lurched, before it moved down.

One floor down and it stopped.

She was forced down another long hall. Doors without windows lined it on both sides. There was writing in strange hieroglyphs that she didn't recognize. Her nose twitched at the faint odor of formaldehyde that permeated the air. Her arms were jerked and pulled back as they halted at a door.

It was the tenth door they'd passed.

She strained to see the buttons that were pressed on a security keypad outside the door. She saw the first three, a nine, eight and four. The last one was blocked from her view. The door opened on silent hinges. Large overhead fluorescent bulbs filled the room with light. No shadows lurked in this space. Everything was lit bright enough that the stainless steel in the room reflected images like a mirror.

Grace was marched to what looked like a surgical table. It took both of the guards to put her on the table. She twisted and turned her body, flailing her arms and legs at her captors until she was exhausted from her efforts. It didn't matter what she did, they were stronger. One put his weight on top of her, while the other restrained her hands and feet with leather straps.

The men left without saying a word.

Grace stretched her head from side to side, looking for an escape. There was none. She wriggled her hands and feet, but the leather didn't budge. There was a table of instruments lined up about a foot away. Her heart beat fast enough to fly from her chest when she focused on what was on the tray.

Scalpels.

Scissors.

Saws.

All were lined up in straight rows. She grit her teeth and renewed her struggle to escape until sweat poured down her forehead. The straps held tight. She was panting and trying to catch her breath when there was a shuffling noise at the door. Her eyes widened as it opened with a quiet swish.

Two men, who looked identical to those who had visited Partlan at the hospital, walked in. They were not dressed in black, and there were no hats or sunglasses to disguise their appearance. They had dark eyes and a slit for a mouth with no lips. There was no hair on their face, eyelids, or head. Their skin was a pasty white color, almost as if they had never stepped out into the sunlight. She clenched her jaw shut against the primal scream that rose in her throat. Partlan had been right.

They were definitely not human.

Chapter 13

A murmur passed between the two creatures who entered the room. They didn't even bother to look her way. Grace swallowed a scream and closed her eyes. Everything Partlan had said was true. The men in the hospital had been aliens. If he was right about that, was he also correct about the need to fear them?

Partlan claimed they were a threat to humanity.

Right now, they were a threat to her.

They walked over to the instrument laden table and ran their long fingers over each tool. It was as if they were counting them.

"You can't keep me here." Grace clenched her hands into fists.

One of the creatures turned to her. "You are with us now."

His lips didn't move.

Grace shook her head. "Who are you?"

"We are here. That is all you need to know." He turned back to the tray and then picked up a syringe.

"Wait." Grace's voice rose to a hysterical pitch. "You can't just jab people without an explanation. What are you going to do?"

"We need your genes." The other creature spoke this time. "It will not hurt."

"I refuse."

"You have been given to us. There is no refusal."

"This is crazy. I'm just an ordinary person. Why would you want to probe me?" Sweat was beading on her forehead. The constant glare of the overhead light was making her skin crawl. She could taste bile at the back of her throat and fear had settled like a rock in her stomach. This was worse than being locked in the closet by her brother.

Much worse.

The restraints were chafing at her wrists, leaving the skin reddened and sore. For a brief second, she wondered if she had the courage to withstand whatever torture they had planned. Partlan had stood firm against Ian. Could she do the same? She closed her eyes and brought up a vision of Partlan in her mind's eye. He was strong and brave. If there was a connection between the two of them, then that must mean she had the same strength within her.

She took a deep breath. "You won't get what you want."

The two creatures turned to her. "We always do. Your words make no sense."

"Poking and probing humans won't tell you anything about us."

"Your genes give us the information we need. Everything about your race is there for our inspection."

"It doesn't explain how we think, or what motivates us." Grace's words were giving her strength. These Albireons, as Partlan called them, might believe that they knew who humans were, but they didn't have a clue.

"We do not need that information." One turned back to the instruments while the other came closer to Grace. "We are able to replicate you. That is all we need to infiltrate and take over."

"We are fighters. Your experiments won't tell you where that comes from."

"Resistance is wasted energy. Only an irrational being would continue in the face of defeat."

"Humans will." Grace grinned. "I told you that there was no way genetics could explain our race. If you try to cage us, we will oppose you."

"We already have control." The creature tilted its head. "You have no need to be afraid. We mean no harm."

"Humans demand freedom."

"We cannot allow that." The second Albireon came close. It had the syringe in its long fingers. "We need your genes and this planet for our survival."

"You want to take over Earth completely." Grace spoke through clenched teeth, careful to avoid their eyes. She hadn't forgotten the effect they'd had on her in the hospital.

"It is necessary. Humans will work for us, once we have total domination."

"As slaves?" Grace didn't bother to hide her contempt. "Why do you need us once you have control of the planet?"

"There are resources that we need."

Grace swallowed back her horror. "What do you want?"

"Water is the most important. Few planets have such a supply as Earth. It is unique."

The creature brought the needle to her arm and pierced her skin. Grace twisted her arm and clenched her fist. She wasn't going to give them what they wanted without a fight. Her arm moved back and forth. The second Albireon reached out to hold her steady, but by then she'd already twisted the needle loose. It clattered to the ground.

"They should have given you the sleeping drugs before bringing you here." There was a sound of frustration in his voice as he bent to pick the syringe up.

"If all you see are sedated humans, then I was right." Grace's tone was smug. "You don't have an inkling about us."

The Albireons went back to the tray. He threw the syringe on it. "You may struggle, but we will get what we need."

"Humans will always fight." Grace tilted her chin. "We will not stand by and let you take over this planet."

There was another murmur between the two creatures and then they both walked over to the other side of the room. Grace's eyes never left them as they moved a large machine with glass tubes and a bank of buttons, from the corner into the center of the room. They turned a few dials and a then a whirring noise sounded.

"What are you doing?"

She had to keep them talking. Stalling for time was part of her negotiation training. The longer they talked, the better chance she had of discovering what they wanted. At the back of her mind was the possibility that Partlan might be able to reach her. She didn't hold much hope of that. Partlan was in the same situation as she was. They were both being held captive and restrained. That meant that she had to rely on herself to get out of this predicament. Talking was the only weapon she had left.

"It would be best if you were not awake."

"So that machine is going to put me to sleep?"

The Albireons turned back to her. "It will ease your anxiety."

"You plan to drug me?" Grace's voice held disdain. "Have you no pride? Is drugging and sedation the only way you can get what you want?"

"It has been useful in the past." The two creatures came back to her. "Are you willing to let us take what we need?"

Grace shook her head. "I've already told you no."

"We want to understand humans." The creature's voice took on an imploring tone. "It will make the transition easier once we take over."

"You expect me to willingly help you control the human race?" Grace almost snorted.

"We are not the only ones interested in your planet." The creature was serious.

"There are more aliens on Earth?" She almost sputtered the words.

"They have tried, but we came to you first." The Albireon who had tried to take her blood picked up another syringe. "Your genetics are fascinating."

"How so?" Grace's eyes were getting heavy. It was a struggle to keep her eyelids open.

"Your genes have numerous codes from other beings in the universe. It is as if you were a combination of many races, not just one."

"Then, we are unique."

"Yes." The Albireon came closer with the syringe. "We need to understand how this came to be."

"Why?" Grace eyed the needle as it neared her. She tried to twist her arm, but it felt weighted down.

"We have to be certain your planet is not a danger to us." The Albireon nodded to his partner who went back to the machine. The whirring noise ceased.

"Our genes will tell you that?" There was a problem with the Albireon's logic, but her brain was too full of cotton wool to pinpoint the issue.

"They will help us." The Albireon was inches away with the syringe. "Also, you are with the Hunter. We need to know why."

"My blood isn't going to tell you that." Grace's tone was dry. "All you had to do was ask."

The Albireon paused. "Ask?"

"It's not complicated. The Hunter is my detainee."

"Hunters are not taken prisoners." He shook his head. "There has to be some control you have over him."

"I'm just a human woman. From the way you people speak, these Hunters are to be feared. So what power could I possibly have?"

"You reasoning is sound."

The two Albireons looked at each other for a few seconds and Grace sensed that there was a silent conversation going on between them. She glanced over at the machine and then back at the tray of instruments. Whatever they were planning involved more than a blood sample. Her body still felt heavy from the drug they had pumped into the room, but the effects were lessening. The best plan for her was to pretend that she couldn't move.

The creatures turned back to her. "There has to be another reason the Hunter does not fight you."

"I am a woman."

"True." There was a tilt of his head. "You are not of the species they were designed to defend. Are you suggesting that they will honor a woman from any race?"

"I don't know. He has sworn to protect women and children."

"So they do not only protect the Kaladin? They have been ruthless in their fighting. We have not done well against the Kaladin and their Hunters."

"He said that you did not respect other races and I have to agree with him."

"We have done no harm."

"You are holding me captive and planning on using my genes for whatever purpose you want. I call that harmful." Sensation was seeping back into her arm. She needed only a few more minutes and then she should be able to continue her struggle for freedom.

"We will release you. We have no plans to destroy your body like the others."

A shock wave rolled through her. The others? These monsters had taken other people and killed them and this was sanctioned by the group that Ian worked for? Grace fought back her nausea.

"Why is Ian's organization working with you?"

"We give them what they need and they let us experiment."

"Do they know what your intentions are for the planet?"

The Albireons shrugged. "It is unimportant to them."

"What did they ask for in exchange?"

Grace forced her voice to remain calm. The longer she talked, the more her strength was returning. The thought of what she would do to Ian and his multi-national organization fueled her determination to survive.

"Technology." The Albireon was matter of fact. "We are more advanced than your planet."

"There has to be more." Sensation was fully returned to her hands. "They probably think they'll be exempt from whatever horrible plans you have for the rest of us. Did you promise them a new home?"

"They wish to travel the universe."

"So they'll escape." Grace fought the urge to shake her head. She didn't want them knowing that their drug was wearing off.

"They have been wise and negotiated." The Albireon raised his syringe. "There has been enough talk."

He took the cap off the needle.

Time had run out.

She had stalled the Albireons as long as possible. Grace clenched her fists and teeth as she pulled up on her restraints with all of her strength. The leather held tight even though the effects of their drug had lessened. She wasn't strong enough to break the straps on her wrists and feet.

She sent a silent cry for help to Partlan just as the needle made contact with her skin.

Chapter 14

Ian was going to die.

He had threatened and hurt Grace.

Grace was his mate and every cell in Partlan's body was dedicated to protecting her. The kiss had been proof of their bond. He had never experienced anything like it before. It had been a physical and spiritual connection. A part of him had reached out and touched the inner core that was Grace. His only regret was that it had ended too soon.

Ian had interrupted them.

He forced his thoughts away from Grace. He could not allow anything to interfere with his task. These men were threatening her. He stilled his mind and focused on Ian. The man would make a mistake. That was all Partlan needed.

Then, Ian would die.

Ian was standing in the center of the cell with his lips pursed. He took one step closer to Partlan. "Any attempt to escape is futile. We hold all the cards, including that lovely lady that just left."

"You are threatening a woman, not cards." Partlan's tone was contemptuous.

Ian shook his head. "I can see that I'll have to talk in simple language to help you understand how serious this situation is. We will kill the FBI agent if you don't give us the information we require."

"If you kill her, then there is no reason for me to speak with you." Partlan's words came through gritted teeth. This man was lower than the worse traitor he had ever hunted. Even thieves had more honor.

"Do you know where she is right now?" Ian's eyebrow rose. "She's in a laboratory being subjected to the painful experiments of one of your fellow extraterrestrials."

"We do not experiment on people." Partlan did not hide his disgust. "We protect people from monsters like you."

"We're doing what is necessary to survive. We didn't invite visitors from outer space. You guys just showed up here. What choice do we have? We make the treaties with those that can help us."

"You are mistaken if you think the Albireons will assist you. In the end, they will destroy your people just like they've done on numerous planets across the universe."

"I follow orders." Ian paced the small cell, his military boots a dull thud against the cement floor. "You're not welcome on Earth. You were definitely not invited."

"We have no intention of harming this planet." Partlan lifted his chin. "There is no reason to hold us captive."

"That's where you're wrong." Ian stopped walking. "I need to know how many of you are on the planet and where you are located."

"A warrior does not betray his brothers."

"We have a large arsenal of methods for extracting information." There was a gleam of satisfaction in Ian's eyes.

"I have endured worse." Partlan shook his head. "You are not the first race to resort to torture. I have been trained to resist."

Ian frowned. "I will have to find another means to convince you."

"You may try, but you will not be successful."

"Why were you running with the woman? Was she your captive?"

"The Sacred Code forbids hurting women. I would never hold one captive."

"There must be a connection." Ian tilted his head. "She's all I need to convince you to talk."

"It will not work."

"I will kill the woman." Ian's voice sounded like steel. "This is not a game. The security of our planet is at stake. You will tell me what I need to know."

"You are willing to sacrifice an innocent woman for this information?" Partlan's tone was scornful. "You have no honor."

"I don't give a damn about honor. I want answers or the woman dies," Ian shouted.

"Then, we will both die." Partlan kept his tone neutral. He had no intention of letting any harm come to Grace, but he was not going to let this man know that. Surprise was what was needed to escape this place, and he intended to use it to his advantage.

Ian smirked. "Where's all your fine talk about defending women?"

"You are the one making the threats. I have only stated that I will not talk."

Ian walked to within a few inches of Partlan.

His face was a mask of anger.

"We'll see how tough you are when I force you to watch the invasive probing of the woman by the Albireons." Ian spit the words at Partlan. "All your talk of honor and it's really your own skin you want to save."

"I have no desire to save myself." Partlan kept his face passive. "Death is a warrior's reward."

"You guys really are insane." Ian's voice was filled with disdain. "What ever happened to survival?"

"We have been bred and trained to be the best warriors in the universe."

"Tell me how many of you there are?"

"I will not endanger my brothers." Partlan shook his head. "I am the only Hunter you will capture."

"We know there's more of you. The Walters spoke of a group who had saved their son." Ian nodded. "We did our research. You were easy to capture and it won't be long before we have the rest."

Partlan's clenched his jaw. He would not give this man the satisfaction of an answer. He believed he knew everything about Hunters, but his words showed his ignorance. A warrior never divulged information. It was only a matter of time before he killed Ian and rescued Grace.

"Don't you have anything to say?" Ian's tone was taunting. "Do you think humans are stupid?"

Partlan gave him a blank stare. "You speak nonsense. I am as human as you."

Ian's eyes widened and he took a step backwards. "You're not from this planet."

"Prove it."

Ian threw his arms up in the air. "I'm not going to stand here and debate this with you any longer. You've tried my patience enough. Now, we'll ask our questions in an atmosphere more conducive to interrogation."

Partlan shrugged. "As you wish. It will not change my answers."

Ian walked out of the cell and motioned for someone to come to him. Partlan focused his mind and tried to connect with Ardal. All he received was silence. He tried again, but the result was the same. Then, he remembered what Eogan had said about the facility blocking signals.

He tried to connect with Eogan. This time he had success.

"Grace has been taken away. Ian says that the Albireons will experiment on her."

There was a long pause before Eogan answered. *"She is probably on level eight. The Albireons have complete control there."*

"I must free her." Partlan refused to consider what would happen if he did not succeed.

"The escape plan is in place. You need to get above ground. The elevator is the only means." Eogan fired his instruction with military briskness.

"Understood."

"If they know you're on the loose, they'll shut down all transport up to the surface."

"I will silence all who stop me." Partlan eased his breathing in preparation for battle.

"Kill them where there are no cameras. Stay close to the walls to avoid being seen. I'll make my way up to the surface and meet you there."

Just then Ian returned with two armed men. They were dressed in grey uniforms with caps on their heads. They looked more like security guards than soldiers, but Partlan had no intention of underestimating their skill. They carried weapons that even an untrained person could use to kill. He would eliminate them before they could fire their weapons. Grace needed him alive.

Partlan moved his neck from side to side and eased his breathing. These men would be easily defeated, but he must do it without others knowing. Surprise and skill were necessary if he was going to rescue Grace and get them to the surface. Failure was not an option.

The cold mental focus of a warrior took over.

One of the men unlocked his handcuff from the cell wall and snapped the free end onto his own wrist before pushing Partlan forward. The other soldier had his gun trained on him. Ian stood at the door with his arms crossed over his chest. Partlan let the man push him another step before he locked his legs in place.

He yanked on the cuffs, pulling the man attached to him, close. He wrapped his arm around his neck and with his free hand grabbed his captor's gun. Before Partlan's next heartbeat, he shot the other soldier dead. Ian's eyes widened and he was reaching for his weapon when Partlan shot him through the heart. Partlan jerked his arm and snapped the neck of the man he was holding.

The body sagged to the floor and he rummaged through the dead man's pockets until he found the key to unlock the handcuffs. Once freed, he picked up the three weapons. One went into the back waistband of his pants, one into his front pocket and he kept the other in his hand. Next, he took the soldier's hat and put it on so that the cap hid most of his face. He shrugged into Ian's jacket and covered his tee-shirt before pushing the bodies along the wall beside the door. If anyone checked through the window, it would look empty.

He edged out of the cell.

The hallway was clear.

He looked up. The camera was pointed high as Eogan had promised. He shut the cell door behind him and edged along the wall making certain he kept out of view. At the end of the hall, there was an elevator and another maze of corridors. The elevator had a large seven on the front.

It was the only way to freedom.

More importantly, it would take him to Grace.

He pulled the brim of the hat over his face and pushed the button. When it opened, he turned and faced the wall. He couldn't risk anyone finding him until after he freed Grace. Escape meant nothing if Grace wasn't with him. He pushed the button for eight. There was a jerk and then he was descending one level. When the doors opened, he kept his head down. He saw the camera ahead and nudged it up with his gun. If they were careful, they should be out of range of the security monitors when they escaped. All he needed was time to get to the surface before the alarm was sounded. After that, he would rely on Eogan's escape plan.

The elevator opened onto three corridors.

They were all identical in appearance.

At regular intervals, there were doors without windows. He would not be able to see which room Grace was in. There was a stillness in the halls, one that he recognized from Cygnus. Everything on this level was soundproof. Each door was heavy enough to prevent noise from filtering out. It was meant to keep their experiments secret, but it was also going to make it difficult to find Grace.

His only option was to try and mind connect to see if she could answer him. He would also try and sense where she was. If that didn't work, he would search every room until he found her. The chances of finding her before the alarm was sounded, were slim.

He leaned against the wall and took a deep breath before focusing. He sent out a mind connect for Grace, putting all of his energy and desire into that reach. Silence was all that greeted him. He tried again. This time there was a faint sensation of a tingling in his head. He focused on that sensation and tried to pinpoint where it had come from.

He turned right.

It was a long hall, but Grace had to be close. He walked several hundred feet before stopping. Grace felt near enough for him to touch, but he still did not have a clear idea of where she was. He opened the first door and looked in. It was a small laboratory, full of glass and steel, but empty. He shut it and went on to the next door, when a sharp cry pierced his head.

He stopped and turned in the opposite direction. He ran past the elevators and stopped in front of another door. It was identical to the all the others in the hall, but there was one difference. This was the room where the cry had come from. There was only one person that he would have been able to connect with like that.

Grace.

Chapter 15

There was a keypad on the door.

He swallowed back his fear and focused on Grace. *"Tell me the code."* Over and over, he repeated his request, until there was a faint response. He swore he heard the numbers nine, eight, and four in his mind. He punched them in. Nothing happened. He tried reversing them. Again, nothing.

He focused on Grace. *"How many?"*

The response was faint, but he heard a four. He needed one more number. He punched in each combination of the three digits with other numbers, until the number eight unlocked the door.

He eased his breathing and readied his weapon.

He flung the door open.

Grace was strapped to a steel table and there were two Albireons on either side of her. One of them had a needle in her arm. Partlan clenched his jaw as he fought to control the surge of anger and disgust that filled him. He slammed the door shut and shot the first Albireon in the head.

Grace's eyes widened and then she twisted her body in an attempt to break free of her bindings. The second Albireon turned toward the wall.

He had the syringe filled with Grace's blood in his hands.

His fingers were a few inches away from an alarm button when Partlan reached him.

He pulled him up by his neck, grabbed the syringe, and shook him. All the pent up fury and disdain he had for the race came through as he gripped harder. They had dared to touch Grace and for that they would die. He held tight until the life drain from the creature and then, he threw him to the ground and shot him between the eyes to be certain he was dead. Albireons were notoriously hard to kill. They drew breath not only from their lungs, but also from breathing holes on their skin.

He would not hurt another human.

Partlan took the syringe over to the sink and broke it. He turned the water on and washed all of Grace's blood down the drain. No one would use Grace's genetic material for their experiments.

"Partlan." Grace's voice sounded weak.

He turned to her. "Are you harmed?"

She shook her head and pointed to the machine in the center of the room. "They used that to pump a sedative into the air. It's made me weak."

Partlan went to the apparatus and pulled the plug from the wall. He made certain it was off before going to Grace. He tugged at the bindings, but they held firm. He grabbed a knife from the instrument tray beside her.

"Do not move."

Grace inhaled. Her eyes were on him as he sliced through the leather bindings. When her hands were free, she rubbed her wrists and waited while he worked on the restraints at her feet. She sat and swung her legs over the edge of the table the moment she was released. Partlan grabbed her to him and held her tight.

"You called to me and I heard."

"Thank God." Grace's voice was a low sob. "I thought you were dead and that there would be no escape from these monsters."

Partlan edged away far enough to look down at her beloved face. He brushed a hand over her cheek and curled her hair behind her ear. Even bruised and covered with dirt, she was the most beautiful woman he had ever seen. His heart should have exploded with the joy that rushed through him as he held her. Instead, it beat strong and steady.

He had found her.

Now, they had to escape.

He cleared his throat. "Eogan has a plan, but we need to get to the surface."

Grace nodded and jumped down. Her body trembled and she grabbed the edge of the table to steady herself. After a few seconds, she straightened up and shook out her legs.

"I'm ready." She walked to the door. "Do you have an extra gun?"

She was a true warrior.

She was perfect.

Partlan grinned as he pulled the pistol out of his waistband and handed it to her. "I did not see anyone when I came to get you. There is a camera at the end of the hall, but I have pushed it upwards. Stick close to the wall and we should be safe."

Partlan opened the door. "Stay behind me."

"I can take lead." Grace tried to move ahead of him.

"It is best that you stay hidden behind me." Partlan was in command mode. "If we are detected on their surveillance they will only be expecting me."

"And you want me to be a surprise."

"It is a simple plan, but effective." Partlan's body blocked Grace as she wedged close to him.

Grace put her hand on his back and stayed near as he sidestepped down the hall.

They came to the intersection where the elevator was located. He pressed the button. The whirling noise let him know the car was in motion. He stood to the side and waited for the doors to open. The car was empty when it arrived. They rushed in and pressed the button for the upper level.

He sent out a mind connection to Eogan. *"We are in the elevator. What do we do when at the top?"*

"I've secured a four wheeled vehicle for you."

"Any guards?"

"Two at the doors to the outside. I've taken care of the two at the elevator. Several truck engines are running. The noise will provide cover." Eogan hesitated a second. *"Above ground is where most of the video surveillance is."*

"How many guards can they mobilize?"

"There are over forty on standby. You need to get out of here as fast as possible. Surprise and speed are your best weapons."

"You will be there?"

"Yes." Eogan's voice was firm. *"Turn right at the elevator. There's a small guard office. I will be waiting for you."*

Partlan braced himself at the door opening. He raised his pistol and steadied his breathing.

Grace raised an eyebrow. "Is there a problem?"

Partlan shook his head. "Eogan is waiting for us above."

The elevator came to a stop.

He motioned Grace to the other side of the door. She nodded and readied her gun. He had no intention of putting her at risk, but it was good to know that she could defend herself if something happened to him. He cocked his pistol as the door opened.

The area was clear.

Partlan stepped out of the elevator and motioned her to stay behind him.

"We better move fast or we'll be overrun with military types." Grace's voice was low.

Partlan nodded and turned to the right. The air was filled with exhaust fumes and the noise of the running trucks. Eogan's cover was effective. The office was where Eogan had said it would be. A large truck was parked in front and blocked them from the cameras.

He opened the office door a crack and scanned the room. Eogan glanced up from the bank of computers he was working at. There were two guards dead at his feet. Partlan motioned Grace to enter and then he shut the door behind them.

"I've sent the video feed into a replay loop." Eogan stood away from the desk. "That should buy you a few minutes."

"We'll need it." Grace leaned against the wall. "What's the plan?"

"There's a fully stocked All-Terrain Vehicle by the side door."

Eogan picked up two guns from the dead soldiers. He popped out the magazines and checked the cartridges before handing the weapons to Partlan. Then, he pulled what looked like a scanner from his inside jacket pocket. He flicked it on and held it out to Grace.

"What are you doing?" Grace jerked away.

"I need to know if they put a chip in you." Eogan motioned for her to hold her arm out and then he scanned it. A loud ringing sounded where the needle had been inserted into her. "We have to get that out."

Grace's expression was dazed. "They took blood from me, that's all."

"They injected the chip first and then let the syringe fill up." Eogan put the scanner on the desk and took out a small black bag from his pocket.

"How quickly can you get it out?" Partlan glanced out the office door.

"It moves up the bloodstream and implants into soft tissue at joint junctures. If we put pressure on her arm, we should stop it from progressing." Eogan unzipped his bag and handed Partlan a rubber tourniquet. "Put that just below the elbow. I doubt it has moved far."

"It happened less than ten minutes ago." Partlan helped Grace out of her jacket and then held her arm. A tremor ran through her and he sent her a wave of calm.

"I'm fine." Grace's voice shook. "We might be able to use this to our advantage."

Eogan scanned her arm again and stopped about one inch from where the needle had been inserted. "Put your thumb just above the area so it doesn't migrate when I cut."

Partlan applied the pressure where Eogan instructed and then watched as he used a scalpel to cut into Grace's arm. Grace's muscles tensed for a second and then relaxed. Eogan used tweezers to poke about the incision. He pulled out a small oval of metal with leg-like protrusions. It looked like a silver bug. He held it up for them to inspect and then put it on the desk.

"I never felt it."

"They microchip every human who comes into this facility, including the employees." Eogan put the chip into a small plastic bag and handed it to Partlan. "It's a precaution in case there's a problem or a prisoner escapes."

"I told you the Albireons were to be feared." Partlan placed a couple of strips of adhesive over Grace's incision. "We can use the chip to mislead them."

"Anything to throw them off the scent." Grace shrugged into her suit coat and flipped her hair over the collar. "We have to get out of here."

"The ATV is ready. I will distract the men while you punch in the security code to open the doors."

"Are you certain you will not come with us?" Partlan

"I'll follow when the time is right." Eogan put the scanner and black bag back into his pockets. "If I leave now, they'll double their efforts to find us. I'll contact you when it is safe."

Partlan shook his head. It was unheard of for a Hunter to deliberately separate himself from his brothers. They worked as a team. That is how they survived. Years of training had made them effective, but then Eogan had not had the same training. To do something alone, was risking failure and death.

"What is the code?" Partlan handed Grace a second weapon.

"Four, eight, nine, three." Eogan opened the door and pointed in the opposite direction. "The side door is at the end of that line of trucks. Once you're outside head north toward the MacDonnell Ranges. When you get through the outer fence, head southeast."

"Why southeast?"

"It's easier to meet up with the road and get to the town. You can also follow the creek bed." Eogan lowered his voice. "The town is twenty miles away and has an airport. That's your best hope of getting out of here before they capture you."

"Anything else I should know?" Partlan eased his shoulder muscles and put an arm around Grace. To lose her before they were free was not an option.

"There's more than one fence around the perimeter. I put wire cutters on the ATV." Eogan pulled a folded paper out of his jacket and pushed it into Partlan's hands. "Here's a map. They patrol the area day and night. Use evasive tactics. The boundary around the facility is prohibited, so if you run into someone, they're either an employee or security."

Partlan nodded. "We will hide until the search quietens down."

"It's desert and mountain. There's some scrub trees and rocks, but not much cover."

"Understood." Grace glanced around Partlan to look outside of the office. "I've had basic survival training for all terrains."

"You'll need it." Eogan slipped through the opening. "Give me the chip. If they spot you, I'll send this off in the opposite direction."

Chapter 16

The sound of gears grinding and then an engine being revved, filled the upper level. Partlan waited until he heard voices yelling from the direction Eogan had gone, before grabbing Grace's hand and moving toward the side door. They would only have a small window of opportunity and he could not waste any time.

Footsteps sounded near him.

They ducked behind one of the large trucks just as a guard ran by them. He was headed toward Eogan. Partlan eased around the vehicle. No one was in sight, so he motioned Grace to follow him to the side door. There was a keypad at the large metal entryway.

"Ready?" He looked back at Grace. "You get the ATV started while I get this open."

Grace pointed to a square shaped, smaller vehicle that was parked away from the trucks. "That one?"

Partlan nodded. "Go."

Partlan keyed in the code that Eogan had given him. The keys lit up and then there was a clicking noise as if a latch were unlocking. There was a loud whirring sound and then the doors slid open about four feet before stopping. It was just enough room to get the small vehicle through. He raced to Grace and jumped onto the ATV that she had already started up. She pulled away with a speed that sent them up in the air before settling back to the ground. He leaned close so that his body would shield her from danger.

They emerged from the side of a mountain.

Partlan squinted to protect his eyes from the blinding intensity of the sun's glare. Ahead of them was a series of white domes and buildings that looked to be the main facility. They needed to head in the opposite direction. Grace turned left and they skirted the edge of a dark reddish mountain until they reached a gorge that headed north.

"This must be where Eogan wanted us to go." Partlan pointed to the opening.

"Are you certain?" Grace looked back at him. "There's a road. That suggests an entry point for vehicles and a gate."

"We will try and detour around the gatehouse."

Grace headed down the road. Partlan sensed her unease, but there was no way around a confrontation. Escape and safety were their priorities. They were on a dirt road inside of the facility, driving a vehicle with an insignia on it. They should blend in.

A small guardhouse was within sight when Partlan noticed another road heading north. He touched Grace's shoulder and pointed. She veered to the left and detoured several hundred yards before the guardhouse. With any luck, they would assume that they were supposed to be there. They continued unhampered until they reached the first fence.

Grace slowed and came to a stop.

Partlan grabbed the bolt cutters and threw a rock at the fence. Nothing happened. It was not electrified. He cut the chain-link fence. They drove through and continued for several minutes until another two fences blocked them. Ten feet separated the last two fences. Beyond the barriers were mountains and desert.

Freedom.

Partlan eased himself off the vehicle and after ensuring it was safe, he made quick work of opening the chain links.

Grace glanced behind her. "Hurry. I see dust from approaching vehicles."

"Drive." He held the links apart.

She sped through the opening. Partlan ran to the second fence, where he repeated the same process. Grace raced through and waited until Partlan jumped on behind her.

"Drive north."

"We don't have a compass."

Partlan pointed in the direction of the mountain range in the distance. Grace took off. Dry, parched land surrounded them as far as they could see. Behind them, billows of dust were filling the air. One plume was where they had cut through the first fence, and then a second billow was coming from the western side of the base.

It was imperative that they reach cover soon. He did not want to chance being tracked by thermal imaging equipment or helicopters. They needed to get as much distance between them as possible.

"They have sent out reinforcements." Partlan spoke above the roar of the all-terrain vehicle. "Gun it."

Grace nodded and even though the vehicle moved faster, their pursuers were still gaining on them. There was no way they could outrun them. Partlan needed to throw them off their track. He scanned the vast desert in front, looking for an area with a variation in topography.

"Turn left here."

"That's opposite of where the airport is."

"This vehicle is too slow. We need to find a place to hide until nightfall."

"You think there is a cave or rock outcrop there?"

"It's our best chance."

Partlan pointed in a northwestern direction. "Head there."

It looked to be a small outcropping of stone. They were still several miles away and beyond that was a drop in the terrain. If he planned it right, Grace would be in hiding before he sent the vehicle off in the opposite direction. He would be within an easy distance to run to the outcrop and yet far enough away from the trajectory of the ATV that no one should guess where they were hidden.

"Stop."

Grace hit the brakes. The vehicle came to a grinding halt within a billow of red sand. Partlan jumped off and opened the storage container. He rummaged through until he found a length of nylon rope. It should keep the engine going when it was tied around the thumb throttle.

"Run to the outcrop and hide. I will catch up to you."

"I can't leave you here alone." Grace crossed her arms over her chest.

Partlan had no intention of wasting time arguing. "If you are captured, then all is lost."

"I can help."

Partlan climbed back on the ATV He handed her two bottles of water and a backpack from the storage. "Getting to safety is the best thing you can do to help me."

A muscle tightened in her jaw. "What happens if you don't come back?"

"Follow Eogan's directions and get to the airport."

Grace glanced over her shoulder. "That's not what I mean. How am I supposed to go on if you're dead?"

The steady beat of Partlan's heart stuttered to a stop. He inhaled a sharp breath. "I will come back to you."

"Men say that, but they never mean it." Grace's voice was low. "You'll leave like the rest."

"I will never leave you, not even in death." Partlan gazed into her deep blue eyes. "You are as necessary to me as breathing. I will always be with you."

"Promise." A tremor ran through Grace's voice.

"Yes. I have every intention of returning to you alive. I need to set up a decoy position so that we can escape."

Grace held his gaze for a second and then nodded. "I'll meet you at the outcrop."

Partlan watched her run in the direction of the rock before turning back to the vehicle. He forced himself to focus on the task at hand. He needed to lead their pursuers in his direction. That was the only way he would be able to keep Grace safe.

He spun the tires of the ATV and kicked up enough dust so that there would be no mistaking where the vehicle was. When the plume had encompassed him, he let the vehicle lurch forward. He twisted the throttle and sent it speeding in a westerly direction.

He drove until he was certain the men from the compound were following. Then he stopped. He set the emergency brake and wrapped the rope around the thumb throttle and tied a tight knot. The engine revved at full speed and when he released the brake, it sped off on its own. Ahead, were miles of uninterrupted desert. The vehicle should continue its journey unhampered.

Partlan backtracked toward Grace.

The ground was hard packed and he made certain he left no footprints. He ran at top speed. For the first time since landing on this planet, he was thankful for his improved speed. He needed to be with Grace. Her words showed that she wanted him near also. It gave his feet wings.

When the outcrop was within sight, his ears picked up the almost silent turning of a rotor blade. He scanned the horizon and saw a sleek black helicopter coming toward him. If they found him so close to the outcropping, then they'd find Grace too. He sent out a mind connection and a wave of urgency to Grace to stay hidden.

He turned away and headed toward a group of low growing scrub trees. It would be difficult for thermal imaging to see him, and he would be hidden from the human eye. He sent a message to Ardal with their location and plans. If he did not survive, Grace needed protection.

He reached the trees just as the helicopter hovered above the rock outcropping.

His breath caught and he sent out another message for Grace to stay hidden. He was too far away to stop them. All he could do was come into the open and force them to capture him instead. He readied himself to jump out when the helicopter dipped lower, throwing up red sand and dust into the air.

The pilot was going in for a closer look.

Chapter 17

He wasn't coming.

What if they had caught him?

Grace slid farther under the stone outcrop until she was at the end of the small cave-like cubby hole. It was barely large enough to hold her body and she had to pull her legs up close to her chest to fit properly. There was a stream of light coming in from the opening and that was the only thing that was keeping her from panicking.

Her body shook with reaction to the horror that she had just escaped. She couldn't bare for them to capture her again. Partlan said that he would protect her, but if they found her in this hole, there would only one thing that would keep her safe.

Death.

She couldn't face going back into the torture chamber she'd just left. It was bad enough that such a place existed on earth, but to think that there were alien creatures who were doing the experiments was beyond what any reasonable person could accept. If she hadn't seen it with her own eyes, she wouldn't believe it.

The whirring of a helicopter blade grew louder. That could mean only one thing. They were getting close enough to land the thing. Once that happened, they would find her. She pulled out her pistol and checked that it was loaded. She counted ten bullets. That meant she had nine shots. She would not be taken alive.

She cocked the pistol and pointed to the entrance. Anyone who came through the opening would be shot dead before their eyes had a chance to adjust to the darkness. She inhaled a deep breath and steadied her hand. There was no room for mistakes.

The noise of the blades grew louder.

Her eyes narrowed as she honed her aim.

Suddenly, a loud explosion shook the earth. She put a hand out to steady herself and looked up at the rock ceiling of her hideout. There was a creaking noise, but no movement. It held in place. The helicopter's engines revved loud and then the noise of the blades was diminishing. The aircraft was moving away. She let out the breath she'd been holding and put her gun down with a shaky hand. She'd been in danger before, but never had she thought about taking her own life.

This was not a normal day at the office.

Nothing was normal since she'd met Partlan.

She wiped the sweat from her forehead with the sleeve of her jacket. The man was larger than life and had turned her existence upside down. She'd had everything arranged. Her career with the FBI was on track and she was up for promotion to supervisor. All she had to do was solve the Walters' kidnapping case and the promotion was hers.

Her ears pricked up at the faint sound of movement outside. There was a scuffling noise and then it stopped. She strained to hear more, but the only sound was the crickets. It must have been nerves or an animal. There was no way that Partlan could have returned from dumping the ATV. She eased the gun down beside her just as the shuffling noise returned.

Before she could raise her weapon, someone had landed on top of her.

She struggled to free herself.

"Quiet." A familiar voice whispered. "They may be able to pick up sounds at this distance."

"Great." Grace sagged back against the hard ground. "One more thing to worry about."

"It will not be a problem."

"Easy for you to say. I barely heard you coming." Grace's voice was a harsh whisper. "What was the loud explosion?"

"Eogan managed a distraction for us."

"Is it safe for us to leave then?"

"Not until nightfall." Partlan edged in closer. "They have two different directions to follow."

"They'll think we've split up."

"That is what I would assume." Partlan took the gun from her. "Did you not hear my mind connection?"

She shook her head. "I was too focused on the explosion and helicopter."

"I tried to warn you."

Grace blew the hair from her eyes. "Everything has gone crazy. Nothing is as it should be."

"There are no rules in combat."

"I'm not talking about fighting." Grace clenched her hands into fists. "It's the kidnapping, the creatures, and the fact that humans are helping aliens experiment on us."

"The Albireons are very convincing."

Partlan's voice was so calm she wanted to scream at him to show some emotion. Instead, she took a deep breath and let go of all of her anger. Partlan's logical thinking had got them out of the compound. She needed a clear head if she was going to help him figure out how to escape this new predicament.

"I will find a way." Partlan's words interrupted her thoughts.

"How did you know what I was thinking?"

"You forget our connection." Partlan's tone was patient. "I heard you call for me when the Albireons were going to hurt you. That is how I found you."

"It still seems impossible."

"Outside of the connection between our fellow Hunters, the pair bond is the most intense. If they mate, that will increase their ability to understand and hear each other's thoughts."

"You mean there's a choice." Grace leaned her head back against the rock. "I thought you just randomly picked someone out of a crowd to be your mate."

"We were chosen to be bonded. There is no understanding why we connect with one woman and not another. I have been near many women since coming to Earth and you are the only one I bonded with."

"That makes me lucky I suppose." Grace heaved a sigh. "Ever since you showed up in Beverly Hills, my life has been nuts."

"For me, it is the opposite." Partlan lowered his voice. "Everything has suddenly made sense. I see beauty all around me and that is because I have bonded with you. You have given my life purpose."

A twinge of joy pinched at her heart, but she refused to give in. If she really was Partlan's pair bond, she needed to be certain that he wouldn't betray her and leave. So far he'd been a man of his word, but years of being abandoned couldn't be forgotten. She was attracted to Partlan, she even believed there was a connection, but she didn't know how far she wanted to take their relationship.

"In time, you will see that I am a man of honor. All Hunters are."

"You're reading my thoughts again." A shiver went through her.

"No." Partlan gathered her close. "Our connection means that I feel what you do. Right now I sense your uncertainty. Nothing, you or anyone does, will break our bond. I am completely committed to you. You are the only woman I could ever mate with."

Grace snuggled closer to him and inhaled his scent. Peace and comfort settled within her. "It's so hard to believe you haven't mated with anyone else."

"It was forbidden." Partlan stroked a hand down her back. "I was bred to obey."

"So, I would be your first mate."

"My only mate." Partlan's voice was a gentle rebuke. "There will never be anyone but you."

Grace eased herself closer to Partlan. There was something in the tone of his voice that told her he was telling the truth. Words failed her as she thought of the gorgeous man who was holding her close. Women would fall over themselves to be in her position. How could she continue to deny her feelings, especially when he had done so much to protect her? She yawned and then covered her mouth.

"I believe you, but it's difficult to accept." Grace ran a shaky hand over his chest. "Men leave me. My father, and then my fiancé. That was the worst. He left me at the altar and I vowed that day to never let myself trust another man. I threw myself into my career and never looked back."

"I vowed to follow the Sacred Code." Partlan was close enough that she could feel his breath against her cheek. "I would never force you. If you have no wish for a mate, then I will honor your decision. We will always be connected, though."

"Can't you find someone else?" Grace's voice held a note of disbelief.

"For me, there will only be you." Partlan cleared his throat. "If you decide to mate with another man, I will still be bonded to you."

"How could you accept that?"

"A woman makes the decisions. We obey her wishes."

"That's how it was on your planet?" Grace faltered on the word planet. It was still too new for her to be comfortable with Partlan being an alien.

"It was until the civil war, and the Holman defeated the Kaladin."

"And ordered Hunters executed." Grace's eyes started to droop and she fought the urge to yawn.

Partlan tucked her head under his chin. "You are tired and should sleep. I will keep watch."

"That's not fair. I can help."

"You need to be ready for our journey this evening." Partlan rubbed his chin over the top of her head. "I am trained to be on guard at all times. It is best you sleep."

Grace yawned. "I shouldn't be so tired. I can't even think straight."

"It is a reaction to your harrowing experience and the sedation drugs you were given. Sleep."

Grace fought to keep her eyes open, but it was pointless. No sooner had she opened one, when the other shut. She drifted off into a deep sleep. No dreams disturbed her until she was awoken by the gentle shake of her shoulder. She stretched her arms above her head and rubbed her eyes.

"What?"

"It is time to leave."

Chapter 18

The night air was cool. Grace rubbed her arms and ran to keep pace with Partlan. They'd been walking for what seemed like hours and her feet hurt. He moved with apparent ease through the rough desert terrain. It was almost as if he could see in the dark. She frowned. Was this something else he hadn't mentioned?

"Can you see at night?"

"Of course." Partlan stopped and she ran into his back. "Do you have night blindness?"

"There's no moon." Grace took several fast breaths. "Everything is an inky black which makes it difficult to see."

"Our vision is improved on your planet."

"Why not? You do everything else better." Grace's voice was a disgruntled mumble. The man was perfect.

"You are tired. We will rest soon."

Grace shook her head and walked ahead. Partlan touched her arm. A spark of awareness flew through her and settled in her inner core. She inhaled a sharp breath as intense desire vibrated within her. A stillness settled between them and she waited for Partlan's reaction.

"Our bond is getting stronger." His spoke in a hoarse whisper.

"You felt it too." Grace's voice trembled. She wasn't a stranger to passion, but this was more than a physical attraction. She sensed Partlan on a spiritual and mental level. They were one.

"It is a powerful connection." He took her hand. "I will not fail to get you to safety."

The sun was hovering on the horizon when they finally stopped. They had reached a road. It was paved and Partlan let her stop to rest. He scanned the area and then led her north of the road and farther into the desert terrain.

"Can't we stay on the highway?" Exhaustion was making Grace's steps less steady.

"It will be watched." Partlan's voice was low. "We will keep it within sight as we travel to the town."

"Do you have a plan?"

Partlan headed toward another rocky outcrop. It was a small cave-like cavern with low growing grass and a couple of short scraggly trees covering the entrance.

"Help will be waiting for us at the airport."

"Eogan?"

"No." Partlan crouched down in front of the cave entrance. "I have contacted Ardal. A team of Hunters is on its way to help."

Grace frowned. "Is that wise? What if the people at the facility capture them too?"

"They will take precautions."

Grace took a sip of water and handed it to him. "You can mind connect over the ocean or was there someone in Australia."

He put the bottle in the backpack. "Distance is not a problem. It is a secret that only Hunters know."

"Should you be telling me?" Telepathic communication would make a military unit more effective. It would be information that anyone trying to capture the alien warriors would want to know.

"You are my pair bond. As our connection gets stronger, our ability to mind connect improves also."

"Do I have a choice?" Grace leaned forward with her arms between her legs. "What if I don't want you roaming about in my head?"

"You may block me." Partlan glanced at the eastern sky and then motioned for her to get into the rock shelter.

"That's why you were always one step ahead of me in finding the boys' kidnappers." Grace got down on her knees and pushed into the cool dark cave. "I never stood a chance against you."

"That is not true." Partlan eased in beside her. "Your background information led us to the perpetrators. From there, it was easy to find the boys."

"Easy?" Grace didn't bother to hide her surprise. "That child trafficking ring had been in existence for years without anyone finding out about them. You and your men found them in a couple of days."

"That is what we are trained to do." Partlan pulled a blanket out of the backpack they had retrieved from the ATV the day before.

Grace pushed her back against the cold stone. The cave was double the size of the one they had spent the previous day in. It was luxurious by comparison, with a dirt floor that would make sleeping comfortable.

"So you traveled the universe saving kidnap victims? Is there really that much crime in space?"

"We right wrongs, wherever and whatever they might be." Partlan stretched out the long length of his body beside her. "We have never had to deal with a trafficking ring before. On Cygnus such a crime does not exist."

"Only humans are capable of such an atrocity." Grace's tone was dry. After ten years in the FBI, nothing surprised her anymore.

"That is not true." Partlan gathered her close and spread the blanket over them. "Look at what the Albireons were about to do to you."

Grace shuddered at the memory. "I won't go back there. Promise you will kill me before you let them capture me."

Partlan's breath stilled for a second. "It will not come to that. I will die defending you."

Grace stretched out the kinks in her legs. "I have ten bullets in my gun. I only plan on using nine. The last one I'm saving."

"Do not speak of such things. I will keep you alive." Partlan's voice was firm. "You need sleep. I will wake you when it is safe to move."

"What about you?" Grace listened to the steady beat of Partlan's heart under her ear. It was soothing. "You haven't had any rest."

"I am trained for this." Partlan ran a hand through her hair. "You have no worries."

She lifted her head off his chest and strained her eyes to make out his face in the dim light of their small cave. He was gazing back at her with a look that caused her insides to twist with love.

Love?

Did she love Partlan?

She inhaled a sharp breath at the thought. Surely she couldn't be serious. There was no way she could have fallen in love with an alien, even if he was human.

"What troubles you?" Partlan's voice held concern.

"Nothing." Grace turned her face into Partlan's chest.

It couldn't be true.

No one fell in love that quickly. Especially in their present circumstances. Danger surrounded them and throughout it, Partlan had been at her side. She had thought she was in love with Travis, her ex-fiancé, but that had been different. There had been no connection between them. They'd shared the same goals, and had both wanted a family, but that was all. She'd mistakenly believed that was love. It hadn't been enough.

"What are you thinking about?" Partlan lifted her chin.

"Travis, my ex-fiancé." Grace didn't bother to lie. Too much had happened for her to hold back the truth now.

"The man who left you?"

"He ran at the first chance he had." Grace's voice took on a musing quality. "It's funny the things you remember. He never once said he loved me."

"He was a fool."

Grace shook her head. "I was the one who was blind. I wanted to find love so badly that I was willing to accept whatever excuses Travis gave me."

"You deserve better."

"I know that now." Grace's voice dropped to a low whisper. "I never knew what love was before I met you."

"You believe in the pair bond." His voice cracked.

"I don't know about that, but I believe in love." Grace stroked her finger down Partlan's cheek. "I've suddenly realized what that means."

She reached up and brushed her lips across his. A jolt of electricity shot through her. She gasped at the intensity, but she didn't end the kiss. She wanted more. She needed to feel and experience everything about this man.

Her tongue stroked his and then the power of their connection took over. Heated desire and wanton need had her pulling at his jacket and shirt. She craved the touch of his skin; to know what his hard muscled firmness felt against her body. Partlan broke the kiss. His breath was coming in gasps.

"What do you want?"

"You." Grace kissed his chin. "I have to know if this is real."

"Show me."

Grace rolled the ends of his shirt up his chest. "Take your top off."

Partlan did as she asked. His hand reached for the button of her blouse. "What about you."

She shook her head. "This is your first time. It should be about you."

Her hand roamed over his firm chest and abdomen, reaching lower until she felt the barrier of his belt and pants. "Take these off too."

"If this is for me, then I need to see you too." Partlan pushed off his boots.

Grace ran a hand over his lower abdomen, luxuriating in the power she felt when he tensed at her touch. The sun was low on the horizon and a streak of light brightened the darkness of their hiding place. It shimmered and highlighted the taut muscles of Partlan's chest and abdomen. The man was gorgeous.

His fingers moved across her waist. "Do you need help?"

Grace shrugged out of her jacket and gathered the edge of her blouse and pulled it over her head. She wore her clothes loose enough so that was all she had to do. She pushed her pants off her hips and kicked her legs free. Partlan followed suit. Soon, they were both naked and facing each other. Grace didn't feel exposed, though.

She had come home at last.

There was no shame or judgement in letting this man see her body.

Partlan's eyes skimmed over her, leaving heat in their wake. She took his hand and placed it over her heart. It beat fast and furious as his fingers brushed her skin and then moved up to her neck. He tilted her chin until she could see his eyes. An inner light glowed from the deep black of his orbs.

Adoration.

Commitment.

A forever love.

A shiver of longing went through her. Never had a man looked at her like that. She melted. She stretch up and captured his lips and let her body and soul lead her on this new journey of love. She didn't care about the danger they faced, or the threat of capture. All she wanted was to be with this man, who claimed her as his mate.

The kiss was a promise.

Grace let the world spin away as she lost herself in the beauty of love. Partlan's fingers caressed her cheek and neck, moving lower until he touched her breasts. His thumb fluttered against her nipple and a sharp, sweet twist of desire settled in her lower abdomen. She ran her foot down the length of Partlan's leg, almost purring when she felt the answering tremor in him.

This was what she wanted and needed.

It didn't matter that they were hiding in a cave, or that they were being hunted by men who would kill them. All she craved was to experience the sensations that Partlan was stirring within her. She had searched for love her whole life and she wanted to experience it, no matter what the future held.

Partlan let his fingers and lips roam over her breasts, licking and tasting every inch of her before he took her nipple in his mouth and suckled. Moist heat flooded her inner core and she groaned.

"Did I do something wrong?" His voice held concern.

Grace shook her head. "It's perfect. Don't stop."

Partlan grinned. "As you command."

He moved to her other breast and his ministrations had her body pulsing with need. She arched her back and reached out to touch him. Her fingers feathered across his chest and then she brushed his nipple. Partlan inhaled a sharp breath as a tremor shook his body. Grace pushed him onto his back and kissed her way up his chest to his neck.

She straddled him and nibbled his lower lip.

"You make me crazy with need." Her voice was a husky whisper. "I want to take this slow, but I don't think I'll be able to."

He framed her face with his hands. "I cannot wait."

She grinned and leaned in for a searing kiss. Their tongues dueled and the heat within her built to a breaking point. She rubbed against him, luxuriating in the shivers of delight that sparked between them. Her body ached for more.

She wanted him deep within her.

To dance with him in the flames of passion.

She stroked his long length as she guided him to her. He was magnificent. She arched her back and eased herself onto him. She held her breath at the wonder of being joined with Partlan. Her eyes locked with his. When he filled her completely, it was as if he'd touched her soul. The beauty of it was devastating.

Shards of bliss exploded within her.

She tilted her hips up and slid down again in a delicious, slow, descent.

Every nerve ending in her body screamed for more. Partlan grasped her hips and guided her movements until she was lost in the motion of their lovemaking. Time ceased to exist. Pleasure rippled through her as she leaned down to kiss Partlan.

He held her close, his lips drinking from hers, stroking and caressing until she was crazed with need. Partlan twisted his body and moved her beneath him, continuing to thrust with an unhurried, steady, penetration that had her on the screaming edge of euphoria. She pulsed with feverish tension until exquisite rapture exploded within her in a shattering climax. Seconds later, Partlan shuddered and collapsed onto her.

Grace trembled with the aftermath of ecstasy that filled her. Never had she experienced such complete fulfillment. The barriers that surrounded her heart gave way and a lifetime of suppressed emotion burst through. Tears welled up in her eyes and she found herself sobbing against Partlan's chest.

"I have hurt you." Partlan's voice was full of distress. He shifted off her and pulled her close.

Grace shook her head and tried to halt her tears, but once the dam had broken there was no stopping it. "You did nothing wrong." Grace's words were interspersed with sobs.

"You should not be crying."

"I need to." Grace clung to Partlan. "Hold me."

Partlan's arms tightened around her. "I will never let you go. You are my mate and there will never be anyone else."

"Promise."

"It is a truth and my vow. A Hunter never betrays his word."

It was several minutes before her tears subsided. Grace was refreshed and cleansed. She hiccupped as the last of her sobs gave way to yawns. She was emotionally drained, but free of the past. She owed that to Partlan. He'd shown her what true love was. She snuggled closer to him and let the steady beat of his heart relax her.

"I love you." She whispered.

Chapter 19

Never had he imagined such bliss. Loving a mate was a delight that he had been denied as a Hunter, but he had no regrets. All the years of fighting and training, had made the wait meaningful. His skills as a warrior would guarantee that Grace was kept safe.

His arms tightened about her.

She loved him.

His heart swelled at the wonder of it. He had never dreamed it possible to have a woman's love or know the delights of a mate. Both had been granted to him, and he was thankful. He brushed a soft kiss across Grace's head. She was fast asleep. They'd walked far last night, but there was still a few more miles of hiking before they reached the airport. His instructions were to wait there for Ardal.

Partlan put Grace's blouse on her shoulders and rested her head under her rolled up pants. He shifted her so that she lay beside him and pulled the blanket over her before getting dressed. He had to be ready in case they were found. It was unlikely that they would be detected in the cave, but he needed to be certain. He wouldn't let anything hurt Grace.

Any pain she felt was his.

He would die defending her.

It had been a close call with the Albireons and he couldn't risk it happening again. It would require all of his abilities as a warrior to see them to safety. Ardal was aware of the danger of this place. They might not be able to help the humans who had already made a pact with the Albireons, but as Hunters, they would make certain that no others were harmed by the greedy and deceitful extraterrestrials.

The hours passed as if in slow motion. The cave was cool, but outside the beating heat of the sun, would have had them dehydrated within an hour. Cicadas could be heard, along with the fluttering wings of a red-headed bird landing in the trees at the cave's opening. Inside, the steady rhythm of Grace's breathing eased his heart.

When the sun moved lower in the sky, he shook her awake. "We need to move."

She yawned. "What time is it?"

"Dusk." Partlan cleared his throat. The sight of her was enough to send a surge of renewed desire throughout him.

"Did you sleep?" She stretched her arms over her head.

"I stood guard."

Grace frowned. "You need rest. Let me take over while you get a couple of hours of shut eye."

"My eyes need to be open." Partlan gathered Grace's clothes together. "I want us to reach the airport before sunrise. Then, I will sleep."

Grace took her clothes and put on her underthings. "How long will it take?"

"Not long. We will stay close to the road. We may be able to get a ride."

"Won't they be looking for us to do that?" Grace pulled her blouse over her head.

"Let's hope they think we've gone north."

"What if they don't believe that?" Grace unrolled her pants.

"Then, they will assume we will try and get to the airport." Partlan kept his voice emotionless.

"So, we may be walking into a trap." Graced pulled on her pants.

"I have made plans for that." A muscle clenched in his jaw. He did not want Grace in danger, but they had to get to the airport. It was their best chance of escape from this place.

"Are you going to tell me?" Grace raised an eyebrow. "I might be able to help."

"I do not want you injured."

"If our relationship is going to survive, you have to trust me." Grace leaned forward. "I've been trained to protect myself and others."

"You are a true warrior." Partlan hesitated a second before continuing. "Once we are at the airport, I will be able to assess our next move. Hopefully, Ardal's team will already be there."

"That sounds reasonable." Grace slipped on her shoes. "Another night of walking. I don't know how much more my feet can stand. These shoes look good, but they weren't made for hiking."

"Just a few hours." Partlan stepped outside and held his hand out for Grace. "This will be a short night, if everything goes as planned."

Grace took his hand and let him lead them away from the rocky hideout. The air was cool now and the sun was below the horizon. He headed toward the road. They continued to follow close to the highway until the lights in the distance signaled that they were near the town.

"Eogan said the airport was south." Partlan pointed in that direction. A glow lit the night sky. "We will go in that direction."

A few minutes later a vehicle pulled up beside them. A young man leaned across the front seat of his truck. "Need a ride?"

"To the airport." Grace went up to the man. "Is that out of your way?"

"You don't sound as if you're from these parts."

"We were out hiking and got lost." Grace grinned. "We should have stuck with our guide."

"I'm headed to the drag strip and that's right beside it." The young man motioned to the back of his truck bed. "Your friend can sit in the box, but you can hop in beside me if you want."

Partlan caught Grace by the waist and lifted her into the box of the truck. "She stays with me."

He jumped up and sat close to Grace. He kept one hand on the side of the truck and one around her.

"You sound jealous." Grace's voice was playful.

"I am not going to let you out of my sight." He motioned to the driver. "He looks harmless, but I will not take a chance."

Grace leaned back into him. "That's alright. I feel safer around you."

The truck pulled into a gravel parking lot twenty minutes later. The sign announced Inland Dragway. The truck stopped and Partlan jumped down. He reached up for Grace just as the driver came around to meet them.

"The airport is over there." He pointed to the east. "Take the road going into the terminal, otherwise you'll run the risk of being on the runway. I don't think any planes come in this late. You're going to have a long wait until morning."

"Thank you." Partlan nodded.

The man shrugged and then head off to the track. Partlan took Grace's hand and walked towards the lights of the airport. The tension in his body increased with each step. If they were going to be captured, the airport would have been one of the first places the agency people would have under surveillance.

"You're nervous." Grace pulled Partlan to a stop.

"The other Hunters are not here yet."

Grace straightened her shoulders. "What do we do?"

Partlan scanned the horizon. "They should be coming in by helicopter, so it would be best if we went to the helipad area."

"Do you have any idea where that might be?"

Partlan shook his head. "There is only one way to find out. We will ask at the airport."

They followed the edge of the roadway that led to the terminal. Partlan kept away from any camera surveillance, but close enough to read the directional signs. There was an Inland Helicopters. It was a place to start. They headed there.

A plane flew in low over their heads and then turned toward the runway. Partlan scanned the area to be certain that there was no other aircraft nearby. The skies were clear of lights. There were no vehicles on the road either. That probably meant that no flights were scheduled.

So who was in the plane that was landing?

He sent out a mind connect to Ardal. "*Have you arrived?*"

"*We are still several miles outside of the town.*"

"*Be advised that we have company. I will scout the area and report back.*"

"*Understood.*"

They kept their bodies low as they came to the first outbuildings and hangars. The runway was lit up, but the only plane on it was the one that had just landed. It was taxiing into a hangar by the time they reached Inland Helicopters. To the side of the office, there was a large helipad.

Partlan flattened his body against the steel exterior of the building and pulled Grace close to his side. "The men from the base are waiting for us. They probably flew in reinforcements on the plane that just landed."

"Now what?" Grace's voice was calm.

"We have the element of surprise." Partlan moved so his body covered Grace. "I will find them first."

"We have to make every shot count." Grace pulled her gun out.

Partlan motioned her to move behind him. "You will only have to use the gun if something happens to me."

"No." Grace spoke in a hoarse whisper. "We both get out of this alive, or neither of us does. I couldn't continue living if something happened to you. Not now."

Partlan turned to her and ran his finger down her cheek. By Cygnus and Warrior, she was beautiful and brave. She was the perfect mate for a warrior. He would not fail her. He brushed his lips across hers and savored the delicious sweetness of her.

"I will be with you always."

"I want you alive." Grace's tone was urgent. "I have finally found love and I'll be damned if I lose it now."

Partlan grinned. "Anger is good. You will be a strong opponent. That will make us invincible against these men."

Grace nodded. "We'll defeat them together."

"You stay behind me at all times. It is the only way that I can protect you."

They inched their way along the wall, and when they came to the corner, Partlan edged his head around the side. The coast was clear. They moved to the next building, and the next, without any resistance. A deep unease settled in Partlan's gut. Years of combat had honed his skills and his intuition had saved his life many times. When they came to the next building, he put his hand out to stop Grace.

"This does not feel right."

"You think they're leading us into a trap?" Grace's voice was hesitant.

"My instinct says we are being lulled into a false sense of security."

"Where are they?"

"There is no sign of them, but I sense that we are being watched." Partlan glanced up at the light posts and edges of the buildings. No cameras were visible. "I am certain we are under surveillance."

Grace exhaled a shaky breath. "So what do we do?"

"You are to stay here and keep out of sight."

Partlan edged back along the wall until they came to a door. He opened it and then scanned the room. It was a small tool shed and empty. He motioned for Grace to enter.

"I want you to stay here."

"What will you be doing?" Grace's voice held a note of suspicion.

"I am going to draw them out." Partlan pulled his second weapon from his waistband. "I will kill them. That is the only way we will be able to escape."

"You can't expect me to let you do this alone."

"It is what I am trained to do."

"So am I." Grace lifted her chin.

"This is not a normal situation." Partlan's voice was firm. "These men do not honor your laws. They will not hesitate to harm you. I cannot allow that."

"So you're going to go storming out there alone?" Grace shook her head. "It is a crazy plan."

"I need to do reconnaissance." He sensed that she was not going to let him do his job. He had to give her a reason to stay behind. "You are my backup. If I am in trouble, then you can come out. It is our one element of surprise."

Grace bit her lower lip and then nodded. "That makes sense. I'll keep a watch at the door."

Partlan released his breath. "I will be back."

He left the room and eased against the cold metal wall of the building. He settled his breathing and heart rate in preparation for battle. He was prepared for however many were waiting for him.

He edged around the corner.

He detected motion near one of the hangars.

It might be a worker, but he was not going to take any chances. He crouched low and ran to the hangar. Two men were standing guard. They wore the same uniform as the men at the base. They were also heavily armed. He stood and eased away from the building.

At the next hangar, at least twenty armed men were waiting. A small jet was there with its hatch open and stairs still lowered. The men were splitting into two teams and gathering in formation.

Partlan backed out and took a deep breath.

He needed to get to Grace.

There was a commotion near the hangar entrance and Partlan moved behind a stack of forty gallon steel containers. The hangar door opened and five men rushed out. They headed in the direction of the other two guards. He stood and eased away from the steel drums. He crept back to the tool shed where he had left Grace.

As much as he wanted to stand his ground and defeat the guards, he needed to keep Grace safe. She was his priority. They were surrounded. The best plan was to wait for Ardal and the others to arrive. As a team, they would defeat these men easily.

Partlan edged closer to the shed where he had left Grace. There was no one in sight, so he tapped and then entered. Grace had a gun aimed at his head. She lowered her weapon when she recognized him.

"Are we safe here?"

"No." Partlan took her arm. "We need to leave. The guards from the base are everywhere."

"We didn't see anyone coming in," she whispered. "The drag way track might be the best place to wait."

"Help will be here soon." Partlan moved out along the side of the building.

They had only taken a few steps when the sound of speeding car engines filled the air. Brakes screeched and then the noise of squealing tires on asphalt as the vehicles skidded to a stop in front of them. The area was swarmed by black Sports Utility Vehicles. There were five in total and they formed a semi-circle that stopped them from escaping.

Dust flew up all around them as a helicopter landed behind the vehicles.

They were trapped.

Ten men jumped out of the cars with submachine guns aimed at them.

Partlan took a step away from the building and pushed Grace behind him. He shot three men dead before they had a chance to get off one shot. Grace's gun sounded beside him. He continued to shoot until he ran out of bullets, with the one pistol. He threw it down and pulled out his second weapon.

Four more men were dead.

Grace screamed beside him. He turned as one of the soldiers from the hangar grabbed her from behind. A knife was at her neck and a second man stood beside her with a gun pointed at her temple. Partlan's eyes narrowed.

These monsters dared to threaten his mate again.

The man holding the pistol against Grace's temple pushed the weapon closer to her head. "Drop your weapon."

Chapter 20

The pounding of Grace's heart echoed in her ears.

The cold metal of the pistol against her head sent a shiver of reality through her. She stared at Partlan and silently begged him not to listen to their threats. He had a chance to survive. All she had done was hold him up. If he hadn't rescued her, he would have been free.

"There is no freedom without you." Partlan's words were clear in her head. *"We will survive this."*

Grace's bottom lip trembled and she bit down on it to prevent her captors from seeing. Partlan had been right. As their connection strengthened, they were able to communicate. She gazed at him and let all the love she felt, show in her eyes. It didn't matter if they survived. She had finally found the forever love that she'd searched for, her whole life.

"Let her go." Partlan held his gun up in the air. "It is me you want."

"We need her for leverage."

"It is a mistake to harm a woman." Partlan's voice took on a note of steel.

"Look who thinks they control this situation." The man holding the pistol to her head chuckled. "You're pretty courageous for a man who's about to die."

"There is nothing brave about death." Partlan sounded bored. "It is inevitable."

Grace sensed the finality of Partlan's words. She couldn't let him risk his life for hers. She wasn't a weak woman. She'd been trained to fight in situations like this and she refused to go quietly. The man holding the knife to her throat had loosened his grip. The one with the gun was more focused on Partlan than her.

A couple of armed men in black suits jumped out of the helicopter onto the tarmac. They were holding weapons and advancing toward them. She needed to make her move now, before they reached Partlan, or all would be lost.

"I can throw the one behind me over my shoulder if you take out the second one."

Partlan didn't blink, not even by a flicker in his eye did she know if he'd heard her. He continued to gaze at her with calm resignation. He'd made a decision; she just didn't know what it was. She took a deep breath and braced her legs. She wasn't going back to that place. They'd have to kill her first.

Her right arm went up to deflect the gun from her forehead at the same time she swung her left elbow up and into the rib cage of the man holding the knife. His arm loosened his hold as he jerked in reaction to the blow. There was a stinging sensation at her throat. She didn't have time to worry about it. She was focused on swinging her body to the side and yanking the arm that held the knife into the air.

She didn't care about the man holding the gun.

Partlan would kill him.

She sidestepped her captor and swung his arm back and then threw him over her shoulder. He went flying down onto the pavement. She stomped her foot onto the hand holding the knife and ground it into the ground. Before he could react, two gunshots rang out. Partlan had hit both men between the eyes.

He grabbed her and pushed her behind him as he took aim at the men near the helicopter.

Shots rang out and the men fell to the ground.

Footsteps, from the side, announced the arrival of fresh troops. They were all carrying guns that were aimed at them. The chance of her and Partlan getting out of this alive were slim, but Grace didn't care. She was with the man she loved. That was all that mattered.

They would go down fighting.

"Retreat to the tool shed." Partlan picked up one of the discarded assault rifles from her now dead captors.

Grace edged back and grabbed a pistol from the ground.

A bullet whizzed past her cheek.

The return gunfire from Partlan was deafening. He was shooting as fast as the men appeared, but it didn't seem to be doing anything. As one man fell, another would appear. She gripped Partlan's arm and urged him back into the building. He stood firm.

"Go." His tone was a deadly calm.

There was no way they would be able to survive this onslaught for much longer. The men from the base wanted them dead or alive. All that mattered was that she and Partlan didn't escape.

A gust of wind blew dirt and stones up into the air. Partlan stopped and pushed Grace behind him. There was no sound, but it was not a regular wind storm. Partlan looked up just as a black stealth helicopter landed in front of them.

"What now?" Grace wanted to cry. The odds continued to be stacked against them.

"Ardal and the other Hunters are here." Partlan pushed Grace against the wall of the building and then aimed at the nearest man coming toward them. "We will be done with these men soon."

Partlan shot the man dead.

The next one was aiming at them, when a bullet hit him from behind. He fell forward and Grace almost gasped at the size of the man coming toward them. He was as big as Eogan, with the same dark hair and eyes. He nodded at Partlan and then turned back to the battle.

Several minutes later, there was silence.

Grace released the breath she'd been holding.

She'd not seen a team of Hunters in action before and it was awe inspiring. The precision and the cold determination of the warriors would have been a terrifying sight to the child traffickers in Caliente. Grace was amazed that any of the criminals had been left alive.

The large Hunter, who had nodded at Partlan, walked toward them. His step was sure. The other men scattered to the outlying buildings. Grace assumed they were checking for more soldiers. The dimly lit tarmac was littered with bodies. The headlights from the empty vehicles added an eerie element to the macabre scene.

Partlan braced his weapon across his chest and walked to meet the newcomer. A silent conversation passed between the two men before Partlan returned to her. He led her by the arm to the helicopter and lifted her in. By the time she was strapped in, the others had returned, and the aircraft took off in a smooth arc away from the airport.

The darkness below was interrupted by the beam of runway lights.

She leaned her head back against her seat and sighed. Her hands were trembling and there was an ache around her neck. Other than that, she was happy to be alive and sitting beside Partlan. They had survived. She reached over and clasped his hand.

"That was a close call."

The large Hunter frowned. "We did not call you."

Grace grinned. "I forgot, you don't do idioms."

Partlan leaned forward. "This is Ardal, our leader. Ardal, this is Grace Kelly, my mate."

Another man shook his head. "Your parents really named you that? I would have been hopping mad at them."

"My father thought it was cute." Grace frowned. "You don't speak like Partlan."

The man held out his hand. "I'm Lorcan. I've been stranded here on Earth, since I was ten, so I'm used to the language."

Ardal sat back with his arms crossed. "We came as soon as we knew where Partlan was located."

"Thank you for saving me too." Grace fell a bit light headed. "For a few seconds there, I did wonder if we might die."

"Partlan is one of my best warriors. He would have protected you."

"It feels good to be alive." Grace sighed. "Where are we going?"

"There is an airport north of here.

Once the helicopter was away from the airport, the interior lighting flickered to life. It was still very dark, but a glow of blue suffused the interior. Grace brushed at the stinging on her neck and winced. Her hands touched a sticky substance. She rubbed it between her fingers and frowned.

"What?" Partlan's voice held concern.

"There's something on my neck." Grace looked up at Partlan. "Does anyone have a flashlight?"

"Here." Lorcan pushed Partlan back and aimed the light at Grace's neck. There was a moment of silence before he spoke. "She's been cut."

Chapter 21

Lorcan glanced over his shoulder. "Ranon, get your medical kit."

Partlan grabbed the flashlight and reached for her chin.

Before he could tilt her head up, Lorcan pushed his hand away. "Don't move her. Ranon will know if she needs stitches."

"How did this happen?" Ardal's voice was a command.

"It must have been the guy I threw over my shoulder." Grace winced as Ranon probed her neck. "He had a knife to my throat."

"It is my fault." Partlan straightened his shoulders. "If I had guarded Grace better, she would not have been taken hostage."

Grace snorted. "It's no one's fault. They took me by surprise. You can't tell me that hasn't happened to you before?"

"Never." Ardal's voice was calm. "We are always in control of a situation. This was different though. Partlan was on his own and protecting a woman in his escape. We should have been there for him."

"Nonsense." Grace inhaled a sharp breath as a cool liquid was applied to her throat. "That stings."

"It is necessary to be certain there is no contamination." Ranon's voice was low. "The cut is deep, but you do not require stitches. I will put some strips on it to keep the incision together."

"Great, all I need is a giant scar across my neck."

"My apologies." Ranon's tone was serious.

"I'm joking." Grace tried to smile, but it turned into a wince as the first piece of tape was put in place. "I've had worse injuries. This is nothing."

"Who has hurt you?" Ardal leaned toward her. "We cannot allow a woman to be harmed."

"It was way before I met Partlan." She had six pairs of eyes staring at her with an intensity that was frightening. They looked as if they were prepared to kill. She edged farther back into her seat.

"I will protect Grace." Partlan spoke in a voice that carried to the front of the helicopter. "She is my mate."

Ardal nodded. "All Hunters have sworn to protect the pair bonds and mates of each other. We were too late this time, but the offender is dead. It will not happen again."

"I'm alright guys." Grace tried to keep the concern from her voice. She didn't know what she'd walked into the middle of, but feuding men wasn't her idea of fun.

"They would never hurt you." Partlan leaned close and whispered in her ear. "There is no need for you to be afraid."

Grace forced the tension in her muscles to ease. She trusted Partlan. He had already proved that he would protect her. If he vouched for these guys, then she believed him. She shut her eyes and relaxed as Ranon continued to work on her wound. The knife had only scraped across her throat. She was lucky it hadn't been deep enough to hit her arteries.

When Ranon was finished, Partlan gathered her into his arms. "Sleep. I will wake you once we are at the airport."

Grace yawned. "If you insist."

When she woke, the helicopter was on the ground. The others had jumped out, which left just her and Partlan aboard the aircraft. She unbuckled herself and waited for Partlan to get out first. He held his arms up for her to hold onto and she descended with ease.

The blade of the helicopter was slowing in rotation and the engine had been shut down. "What's going to happen to this?"

Partlan shrugged. "It is not our concern. It was borrowed."

Grace stopped. "They stole it."

"It was necessary." Partlan coaxed her to the small jet that was waiting in the center of a small airstrip.

"Is the plane stolen?"

Grace had to run to keep pace with Partlan. She had never committed a crime before she met Partlan. In the space of a week, she had broken the law so many times that she was beyond redemption. It didn't matter that none of this had been of her choosing. Everything they had done had been necessary to stay alive.

"The plane is ours."

"How can you guys afford it?" Grace let Partlan lead her up the stairs to the interior of the jet.

"It belonged to Lorcan's unit." Partlan led her to a seat beside one of the windows. "They were mercenaries before joining Ardal."

"And you aren't?"

"No." Ardal interrupted their conversation. He sat down in a seat across from them. "We are Hunters, even on this planet. We right the wrongs we are asked to."

"But you do it for money."

"Not always." Ardal leaned forward. "People contact us to help them, and we do. They know that we are not limited by the laws of this planet. Only the laws of the Sacred Code bind us."

"And those laws include not hurting woman or children." Grace shook her head. "That's almost impossible to enforce."

"Once we look into an injustice, it will not happen again." Ardal looked over at Partlan. "Men who kidnap children should not be left alive. If a woman had not asked for their lives to be spared, they would be dead."

"I understand, but that is why we have laws."

"Was not one of those men a judge? If the people who enforce your laws are corrupt, then people have no choice but to ask us to get justice for them."

Grace rubbed her forehead. As much as she agreed with what Ardal was saying, she had sworn to protect the law. She didn't know if she could give that up just because she had found love. It was a difficult decision, but one that she would have to make. A thought suddenly occurred to her.

"Are we still in danger because of those agents at the facility?"

Partlan looked over at Ardal, before he spoke. "They will hunt us down until we have been killed." He was matter of fact. "We cannot let them find us."

Grace's stomach dropped. "That includes me."

"What happened at the facility?" Another man sat beside Ardal. His voice was a growl. "How did they find you, Partlan?"

"This is Darrogh." Ardal pointed to the newcomer. "He is the second in command of the unit."

"Why were you taken captive? Did the woman cause it?" Darrogh fired his questions like bullets.

"You will have to forgive Darrogh." Ardal cleared his throat. "He has not found his pair bond and has no understanding of the depth of the bond between mates."

"A warrior has no use for a mate." Darrogh crossed his arms over his chest.

"No one can fully appreciate it until they have a mate." Partlan's voice was low. "I was not blind to the connection between mates. Darrogh refuses to understand."

"To answer your question Darrogh, I was not the reason that Partlan was taken to Australia." Grace used her most official FBI voice. "Partlan was visited by two strange men in the hospital and I happened to be there with him at the time."

"Albireons." When Partlan said the word there was silence from the other men.

"Are you certain?" Ardal frowned. "We eliminated them in the Cygnus system. The Kaladin would not do business with them because of their deceitfulness."

"There is no doubt." Partlan gathered her hand in his and a wave of calm ebbed through her. "Grace was taken away to one of their labs."

"They injected a chip into me." Grace held out her right forearm. The bandage had long since disappeared, but the small incision where Eogan had removed the chip was still there. "It's been removed. That is the only way we were able to escape. Otherwise, they would have tracked us."

"How did they gain such power on Earth?" Ardal's voice held disbelief.

"They had full rein at the facility. Eogan was very clear about that." Partlan moved closer to Grace.

"Who is Eogan?" Darrogh's eyes narrowed with suspicion.

"He helped us." Grace spoke before Partlan could explain. She didn't want anyone to be angry with the Hunter who had risked his life so that they could be free. He deserved all of their gratitude.

"Eogan is a fellow warrior who arranged our escape." Silence followed Partlan's words. "He is clan Rioge and has been stranded on Earth as long as Lorcan and the others."

"Impossible." Lorcan shook his head. "He's dead."

"The humans kept him captive and altered his implants." A hush fell over the plane at Partlan's words.

"Why didn't he contact us?" Lorcan's eyes widened.

"That is not possible in the facility. Eogan thinks there is something that blocks frequencies and is interfering with our mind connection."

"What about when he was away from the base?" Lorcan frowned. "We would have come for him."

"He was not allowed to leave for many years, and by then, he had been informed that all Hunters had been killed."

"So, he made no effort to escape." Ardal nodded. "I am amazed that there is another of my clan still alive."

Lorcan sank into a seat across the aisle. "He was captured with Catal, but we thought he was dead."

"Horrible things were done to Catal." Partlan's voice was solemn. "They were done to Eogan also."

"Isolation from his brothers would have been bad enough." Ardal's jaw tightened. "What else have they done to him?"

"He is used as a killing machine for them." Partlan's gaze held Ardal's "I believe he was sent in to kill the people at Selena's compound in Colombia."

"Why has he not escaped?"

"He has implants that are active." Partlan rubbed his forearm. "The humans have figured out a way to control him."

"The Albireons have probably helped." Ardal's tone was scornful. "We must rescue him."

"He says not to try." Grace's voice was soft. "He will come out when it is time, and then he will contact you. He fears that all of the Hunters would be killed trying to rescue him."

Ardal nodded. "He is clan Rioge, so he must have considered all options. We will wait for him to contact us."

"That is what he wants." Partlan brushed a finger over Grace's hand. "He doesn't want an immediate attack on the facility either. He thinks they will suspect him of helping with our escape."

"That makes no sense." Darrogh's tone was derogatory. "The Albireons know that Hunters never rest until they have accomplished their mission. Kidnapping one of our own, is enough reason for us to retaliate."

"Think about Eogan." Ardal was the voice of reason. "He has been a captive since he was a child. They probably have no reason to suspect that he would turn on them."

"Eogan had never considered disobeying until he sensed that I was near." Partlan pursed his lips. "He felt that he was the only Hunter on this planet and with no hope of returning to Cygnus, why would he escape?"

"True." Ardal nodded. "Also, from what Catal told us, he and Eogan were ordered to be captured. They were used as bait so the others could go free."

"Eogan had been told that all the others who had landed on the planet had been killed. The humans might not know about the mind connection, but they certain did not want Eogan looking for survivors."

Grace sighed. "It is a horrible thing to think that humans would do such a thing."

"We are human too." Silence followed Ardal's words.

"That will take some time to digest." Partlan was solemn. "This world has felt so strange, but now I know the truth. This is where we belong."

"Especially since you have found your mate." Ardal spoke with approval. "There is no way to describe how wonderful that is."

"I have seen how it changed you and the others." Partlan's voice was respectful. "It made me yearn for something I did not understand, until I found Grace. Now everything makes sense, including why we were transported to Earth for execution."

"And why we were sent to train here as children," Lorcan added. "For years, I despised the humans for what they did to my fellow Hunters."

"The humans had help." Grace's voice faltered as she remembered the horrors that she had seen in the facility.

"The Albireons." Lorcan nodded. "Now that we know they are behind this, we will be better prepared."

"They hold a lot of power on this planet." Partlan's tone was cautious. "Eogan says that the group that works with them in secrecy, controls most of the world's assets. They have more power than individual nations."

"We must proceed with care. There will be no movement against this group until we have all the information on them."

"Or until they attack us." Darrogh's voice was harsh. "I do not think we should wait for them to come to us. The sooner we plan what to do, the better."

"Perhaps." Ardal's voice was calm. "I will take your advice into consideration. Right now, we need to give Partlan and his mate some rest. They have been through a harrowing experience, and I suspect Partlan has not slept."

"You're right." Grace smiled up at Partlan. "He refused to sleep and kept watch the whole time."

"We have several hours before out next stop." Ardal stood. "We will leave you alone."

"Where are we landing?" Grace reached for a blanket that Darrogh held out to her.

"It is a secret location that we have used in the past." Lorcan crossed his arms.

"Will I be able to contact my colleagues in the FBI and let them know I am safe?" She opened the blanket.

"I will permit only one call from the airport where we refuel." Ardal's voice was firm. "After that, if you chose to come with us, then contact with the outside world is forbidden."

Chapter 22

Their plane was circling the area where they were going to land. It was little more than a long strip of flat ground in the middle of miles and miles of forest. They had refueled on the west coast and Grace had been allowed one phone call.

Now, they were in an isolated location at the edge of what was known as the Ring of Fire in Canada. No one frequented this area except mining firms. Lorcan had set up a company as cover. He had mineral rights for huge sections of land, and had bought everything that had been available. They would be safe and inconspicuous here.

It was a long way from Los Angeles.

She sighed and then rubbed her eyes before stretching her arms over her head. "It looks pretty secluded. How soon before we're on the ground?"

"A few minutes." Partlan's voice was hesitant. "We need to talk about you staying with me."

Grace's heart stuttered to a stop. "You don't want me."

Partlan shook his head. "I need you always. I do not wish you to be forced into a decision. This is a difficult life we lead."

"The life I had before is gone." The tight band around her chest shortened. "There are few choices left to me."

Partlan nodded. "You believe you have to remain with me."

"That's not what I said." Grace straightened away from the window. "I love you. If being with you means giving up the FBI, then so be it."

"You are certain this is what you want?"

Grace tilted her head. "Are you having second thoughts?

"Never."

Partlan leaned down and kissed her. The world spun away and all of her doubts and concerns vanished. This was where she belonged. Whatever the future held for her, it was better than what she had left behind. She'd gladly sacrifice a career in law enforcement to be held and loved by Partlan always.

The plane landed without incident and they parked it inside a hangar hidden by trees. This was a private airstrip that Lorcan had created years ago. No one could search it, or see what was here from the air. It provided security and secrecy. Grace admired the forethought that had gone into the operation.

There were two green camouflage painted SUV's waiting for them inside the hangar. Ardal was the first to disembark. As soon as the hatch opened, a woman jumped out of one of the vehicles and rushed into his arms. Ardal picked her up and kissed her. They walked hand and hand to the first vehicle.

"Who is she?"

"That is Fiona, Ardal's mate." Partlan stood and waited for Grace to go in front of him.

"How many Hunters have found mates?"

"Four, including me."

"That's not very many."

"We have only been here for ten months." Partlan spoke close to her ear. A shiver of awareness danced across her neck.

She grinned and looked back at him. "I would have expected big boys like you to have taken the females by storm."

"It does not work that way for us." Partlan frowned. "There is a reason one's mate is chosen. Some may call it destiny. I believe the mate that is our perfect match, is the one we find."

"Well, I would hardly call myself a great catch for a warrior type." Grace's tone was derisive.

"You are wonderful." Partlan's voice rose in awe. "You are a true warrior. There is no one I would rather have by my side."

Grace almost missed her step. She had always considered herself too tall and gawky for most men. To hear that Partlan considered her perfect was a surprise, especially when she watched the petite redhead that was their leader's mate. Even her ex-fiancé had told her that she wasn't what most men wanted.

"So what happens now?" Grace cleared her throat. "Is this like witness protection and we have to hide for the rest of our lives?"

"I have work to do. I cannot hide." Partlan took her elbow and led her to the second vehicle. "We will discuss it more at the cabin."

Grace shrugged. "As you wish."

She'd already spoken to Bakker and he'd informed her that the bureau thought she was dead. That left little chance of her resuming her career in the FBI, assuming she wanted to go back there. She'd changed since meeting Partlan and the kidnapping. She wasn't willing to accept the status quo's perception of what was happening in the world. There was much more going on behind the scenes.

"I can't go back to the FBI. Where does that leave me?" Grace's words were out before she'd thought about Partlan's reaction.

Partlan held the door of the car open and waited until she was seated before getting in beside her. "You can help with our work."

"How?" Grace clasped her hands together on her lap. "I'm not strong like you and the other Hunters. I don't have the ability to mind connect either."

"You know law enforcement on this planet." Partlan took her hand and squeezed. "I would like you to stay and be my mate, but if you do not want this, I am sure we can set you up with a new life; a life that you could be happy with."

Grace's heart constricted. "I will only be happy, if I am with you."

Partlan stared at her for a second, his eyes unwavering in their look of adoration. Grace fought back her own tears of joy as she let him gather her into his arms. His kiss was a vow. His lips tender until the heat of their need took over. The world disappeared and it wasn't until another Hunter cleared his throat that she realized they'd been joined by a stranger.

"We have arrived at the cabin." He seemed to be younger than the other Hunters that she had met on the plane.

Partlan grinned. "Meet Firbin."

Firbin turned around from the driver's seat and held out his hand. "I am glad to see that Partlan has found his mate. He's one of the best warriors in our unit."

"Thank you." Grace's face flushed with embarrassment. "I forgot others were in the vehicle."

"No problem." Firbin opened his door and jumped out. "I understand the pair bond is an intense thing."

Grace looked at Partlan, but he only shrugged. She slid over the seat to the door and exited the vehicle. They were in a densely wooded area with what looked like a large log cabin hidden under the trees. Partlan led her to the cabin door.

The cabin was huge. There was a central area, with chairs and couches scattered about. A large fire pit, in the middle, made it look more like a ski lodge than a hideaway. From the main area, three hallways extended. One led to an open kitchen and a large dining room. The other two were dark hallways, and Grace assumed that they led to the sleeping quarters.

"How many live here?" she whispered as she turned to Partlan.

"As many as necessary." Ardal's voice boomed from the main lounging area. "Come and meet my wife. She has been waiting anxiously to see you, ever since Partlan communicated that he had found his pair bond."

Partlan pressed a hand to her back and urged her forward. Standing beside Ardal, was the woman she had seen on the airstrip. At close range, she could see how beautiful Fiona was, with flowing red hair and lively emerald eyes. When she reached them, Fiona hugged her.

"I'm Fiona." She stood back and smiled. "It must be so confusing for you right now, but I promise everything will get better."

"Fiona rescued us when we crash landed on this planet," Partlan explained. "We owe her much."

"She also trained to be a medical doctor, so she can look after you." Ardal's voice held pride.

Grace touched her throat. "Ranon fixed it."

"He is clan Leigh. They are gifted in healing." Partlan motioned for her to sit on the chair beside him."

"How did you get it?" Fiona sat across from Grace.

"I had a knife held to my throat and when I threw him, he cut me."

Fiona's eyes widened. "You did this on your own."

Grace shrugged. "I'm trained in martial arts and self-defense."

"I was not quick enough to prevent the injury." Partlan's voice was full of regret.

"You were too busy killing the other men who were shooting at us." Grace rolled her eyes. "You had enough to do. I was able to handle the situation."

"I understand what you mean Partlan. Your mate is indeed a warrior at heart." Ardal sat forward. "If you choose to stay with us, we can use your skills to help others."

"What exactly do you do?"

"We right the wrongs that others have suffered." Ardal's voice was serious. "They contact us through the internet and tell us what has happened. If there has been dishonor, or the Sacred Code is broken, then we will get them justice."

"That is how I contacted them." Another woman's voice sounded from one of the hallways. Grace looked up and recognized Selena Duarte. She had been the nanny to the Walters' son Gates. Selena's son, Tarrin, had been kidnapped with Gates and sold to child traffickers. All of her FBI intelligence had led her to believe that Selena was somehow involved in the kidnaping.

"I owe you an apology about the kidnapping." Grace stood. "I'm glad to see you're alive and well. I didn't want to believe that you might be involved in hurting the children, but it was my job to pursue all angles."

Selena's face softened. "I wasn't completely honest. I didn't tell you that Catal was Tarrin's father. That might have helped you see things in a different light."

Grace shook her head. "I would have suspected him."

"When your legal system makes mistakes, people are hurt." Ardal spoke now. "That is why they come to us."

Selena and Grace both sat.

Grace's apology had eased the tension between the two, but she sensed that it would take time before they would be comfortable with each other. Grace turned her attention back to Ardal.

"I have spent many years ensuring the law is followed. The system isn't perfect, but we make a difference." She looked down at her hands. "A great many people who have committed atrocities are behind bars because the courts did their job."

Partlan put his hand over hers. "We handle them differently. If someone is guilty of harming another, we do not give them another chance."

"Our experience shows that these individuals will not change." Ardal's voice was serious. "If they break the Sacred Code, then they will be put to death."

Grace inhaled an unsteady breath. "It's hard for me to throw away so many years of training."

"We aren't asking that of you." Partlan leaned closer. "All I ask is that you stay with me."

Grace looked up at him and melted. "That's a given. There's nowhere else I want to be."

"Then, we have no problem." Ardal leaned back in his chair. "You are Partlan's mate and one of us."

"Hurray." Fiona's gave a short cheer. "I'm happy to have another woman in this circle of men."

"Me too." Selena nodded at Grace.

"Thank you." Grace's heart filled with gratitude. These people had accepted her unconditionally because of Partlan. "I want to help with your work too."

"Good." Ardal stood and held his hand out to Fiona. "We could use the expertise you have about the law enforcement on this planet."

"I'll explain the finer points of living with a warrior after you've settled in." Fiona took Ardal's hand. "You're lucky. When I was first mated with Ardal, there were no other women for me to talk to."

Selena stood. "I will help as much as possible, but I've only been here a few days."

"Where are Catal and Tarrin?" Ardal frowned and looked about the large room.

"Catal is training Tarrin outside. They should be back soon."

Ardal nodded and then turned to Partlan. "Take your mate to the room at the end. That will be your space. She looks exhausted."

"I'll try and find something for you to wear." Fiona looked at Grace with a frown. "I don't think we can salvage those clothes."

"Maybe one of my tops will fit," Selena tilted her head. "Any pants we have, will need to be lengthened."

"Leave it to us." Fiona's voice was hopeful.

Grace privately thought it would be a task beyond anyone's capabilities. They were in the middle of the bush, and there were no stores. She was taller than most women. She wasn't model thin either. Perhaps a thorough cleaning of the clothes she was wearing would do. Right now, she was too exhausted to care.

Partlan seemed to sense that and he stood and pulled her up beside him. Together, they left the others in the great room and walked to the room that had been assigned to them. Partlan opened the door and let her enter first. It was sparsely furnished, but warm. There was a door opening off the main area. It had a mirror that showed a toilet and shower in its reflection. Grace rubbed her arms and sighed. Finally, a comfortable place where they could be alone.

"Should we toss a coin to see who gets to use the shower first?" Grace turned to Partlan as he shut the door. "I'm willing to wait for you, just don't use all the hot water."

"You will go first." Partlan gathered her close. "I would never dream of letting my mate wait."

"Promise?" Grace gave him a teasing kiss.

"Always." Partlan's voice was serious.

"I think I'm going to like this mate thing." Grace wiggled out of Partlan's embrace. "I'll hurry. As nice as kissing you is, a shower is what I need most right now."

Chapter 23

Grace was lying naked under the covers.

Partlan was still in the shower and she was waiting for him to come out. It had only been a few minutes, but the anticipation was killing her. Never had she hungered for a man before. She needed him with a gut twisting desire.

The water shut off.

Partlan entered the room.

A towel was wrapped around his waist leaving his chest bare. Droplets of water clung to the fine hairs that were scattered across his chest. Grace's heart pounded at the sight of him. He was perfect, with broad shoulders, solid muscles, and a chiseled abdomen. She sat up in the bed, holding the sheet against her chest with one hand and patted the bed beside her.

"Come sit with me."

Partlan raised an eyebrow. "Is that all you want."

"You know it isn't." Grace could barely keep the impatience out of her voice. "I need you now."

"I am yours to command."

Partlan dropped his towel.

Grace inhaled a sharp breath as the full extent of his arousal was evident.

"Hurry."

Partlan grinned and then got under the covers with her. The smell of soap mixed with the scent that was Partlan, surrounded her as he pulled her close and kissed her. His tongue licked and his teeth nipped until he had her in a frenzy of need. Only then, did he relent and caress her with his fingers. Tingling, teasing, and tantalizing every inch of her body. She groaned with the pleasure of it. It seemed ages since they'd last been together. So much danger and death, but now there was only the two of them.

Grace stroked down Partlan's back, feathering her fingers across his skin. His groans of approval gave her a sense of empowerment and she moved lower, urging him to come closer.

He didn't disappoint.

He positioned himself and then entered her in one swift motion.

She was in heaven. Sensations of bliss and pleasure roared through her body. Every nerve ending was on fire as she enclosed and tightened about him. This was the man she loved. She had never experienced such completeness in her life before. He'd promised to be with her always and she trusted him.

"You are the only woman for me."

"I love you." Grace shuddered at the beauty of the moment.

Partlan brushed his lips against hers.

Then, he thrust deep.

The world spiraled out of control as they moved. They found a rhythm that built their desire until they were riding on the edge of the precipice. They were connected on a spiritual and physical level that held them in the throes of passion. They existed as one and together they exploded with ecstasy.

Tiny shudders of bliss continued to ripple through her as she drifted back from the heights of pleasure. Grace let the completeness of their loving envelop and comfort her. She lifted her face and kissed Partlan. A kiss filled with promise and thankfulness. He was her mate and she was truly blessed.

"Thank you for being with me." Tears filled her eyes. "You risked your life to help me escape. That is more than anyone has ever done for me before."

Partlan's eyes were filled with adoration. "You are the one who has given me so much. I never dreamed that I would know the wonder of a pair bond."

"It's more than I expected." Grace sniffed back her tears. "Every man I've ever known has left me, but you have shown me that there are forever men."

"Does this mean that you will truly stay?"

Grace nodded. "I could never leave you."

"Will you be my wife?" Partlan's voice was hesitant. "Ardal and Fiona are legally joined in marriage and I want this for us too. I want everyone to know that I am yours completely."

Grace couldn't believe her ears. They had known each other for so little time, but it felt right. She'd been down this road before with her ex-fiancé and that had ended in disaster. Now, she knew how wrong they had been for each other. She was thankful that he'd had the courage to walk away and leave her free to find Partlan.

Partlan frowned. "Did I not say it right?"

"You said it perfectly." Grace wiped her eyes. "I would be honored to be your wife. To wear your ring and let the whole world know that you are my husband; the man I love."

Partlan gave her a tender kiss. "We will have to ask Lorcan to give us identification so that we can do this legally, according to the laws of your land."

"I don't care how we do it. I just want to shout it from the rooftops that we are one."

Partlan grinned. "That might not be the best plan. There are still people looking for us."

"Will we be safe?"

"Yes." Partlan's voice was definite. "As long as you are my mate, all my brothers will protect you. No one will be able to kidnap you again."

"That makes me feel protected." Grace frowned. "How will we stay hidden?"

"We are part of your world, but outside it. We have computers and equipment that have been altered to avoid detection. Many of the skills and knowledge that we have from Cygnus are helpful to us now."

"It sounds like a crazy lifestyle."

Grace heaved a sigh. It was no different from the life she'd left behind. Working for the FBI had meant that she could be transferred at any time. Her field work could be in any state, and she was at the whim and mercy of her superiors. She had never considered it a problem, but looking at it from her new life on the run, she realized that she really didn't have much to leave behind.

"Will that be a problem?"

"No. I'm used to moving around. I just want to be certain that I'll have a purpose. I need to work. I hate being at loose ends."

"There will be no ends." Partlan's tone was severe.

"It's a saying. It means I'll have time on my hands and I'll want to do something." Grace smiled and stroked a finger down Partlan's cheek. "I'm really going to have to teach you about the English language."

"That would be useful." Partlan nibbled her fingertip. "We had to download Earth languages as we were crashing. The computer failed before it had finished giving us all the information. We have the basics only."

"Hmmm, that sounds dangerous." Grace brushed her lips across Partlan. "We'll have plenty of time to talk about it later. Right now, I want to do something else."

Partlan grinned. "It is time for us to bond again."

"I thought you'd never ask."

Partlan captured her lips in a kiss that seared right to her soul. His tongue and fingers caressed and teased her until she was a mass of molten desires. Only then, did he join with her and they began the dance of loving that was unique to them. All through the night, Partlan showed Grace how powerful and tireless his lovemaking could be. It was the early hours of the morning before she fell asleep, satiated and exhausted.

Chapter 24

Partlan eased out of the bed and stood for a few minutes watching Grace sleep. She was exhausted after their ordeal and he had not let her rest much last night. His eyes lingered on her neck and he fought back his anger at the wound she had suffered. If only he had taken better care, or been quicker.

Grace wasn't bothered by it though. She said it was minor compared to some of her other injuries. She was a warrior and his heart swelled at the realization that she was truly his mate.

A wonderful world of purpose had opened up for him. By Cygnus and Warrior, he was grateful to have been given the gift of a pair bond. It was a miracle and a privilege to know the joys of a mate. He had been truly blessed.

Now, he must be certain that no harm would come to her.

He could not bear it if she should be injured again. She was his responsibility despite her training. He was a Hunter; the elite of all warriors. He would protect her with his life. He took one last look before leaving. Outside the door, there were some clothes laid on a chair. He picked them up and put them inside their room. She would want to dress before coming to meet with the others.

In the kitchen area, Fiona was busy making breakfast. Firbin was at her side helping and Ardal was sitting at the table talking with Catal. Lorcan was hunched over a laptop computer beside them, and Selena was pouring coffee. When Partlan came in, Ardal, was the first to look up.

"Are you ready for work?"

"Yes." Partlan pulled out a chair and sat. "I left Grace sleeping."

"We need to discuss what happened in Australia."

Partlan nodded. "The Albireons seemed to be in control. Not only do we have to protect people from themselves, but from threats from other planets."

"How long have they been here?"

"Eogan said that it had been over seventy years." Partlan smiled up at Selena when she handed him a cup of coffee. "The

Albireons exchanged technology for free access to humans for experimentation."

"What can they possibly want with the humans?" Lorcan looked up from his computer. "I can find no mention of this facility, except that it monitors satellites. There is some chatter about it being a covert surveillance site that mines electronic data."

"Why in that location?" Partlan took a sip of coffee.

"Because it's too far inland for anyone else to spy on it." Grace's voice came from the kitchen door. "Nobody can station ships in the waters around Australia and spy on them. It's the perfect location for clandestine activities."

Partlan stood and pulled out the chair beside him. Bruises were evident on her neck. Her step was firm, though. She had put the clothes on that Fiona and Selena had given her and she looked stunning. The shirt was tight, but it showed off her curves. Gone was the loose business suit and in its place a more casual and relaxed look.

Grace sat. "The Albireons who held me captive insisted they wanted the human genetic code. They needed us for survival even though they had already infiltrated the planet."

"That's insane." Lorcan's voice was outraged. "When did this happen and why?"

"It's been going on for years." Grace cleared her throat. "I'm afraid individual humans have been helping them with the hope that they will have a part of the profits when the Albireons take over."

"Humans are helping them?" Fiona put a plate of muffins on the table. "Do you know who?"

"Eogan said that some of the oldest organizations and families with money had made a treaty with the Albireons." Partlan handed Grace a coffee. "They are not connected with any one government."

"So they have gone above the law?" Selena shivered. "That is more frightening than thinking that a government is responsible for the outrageous things they are doing."

"I agree." Grace's voice was crisp. "I would like to shut them down if possible."

"If it is a world organization then that might be impossible." Ardal's voice was matter of fact. "We can work against them, but to defeat the Albireons when they have infiltrated a society to such an extent is difficult."

"I want to make certain they stop kidnapping humans and experimenting on them." Grace shuddered. "It was horrible to be held captive. There was no way to stop them from doing whatever they wanted."

Fiona came over to her and clasped her shoulder. "I know how bad that can be. I was stalked, beaten, and almost killed by one of my medical instructors. I had to leave my life behind and go into hiding and he still found me. If Ardal hadn't rescued me, he would have killed me."

"You understand why I don't want that to happen to anyone else." Grace looked up at Fiona. "I'm trained in defending myself. What about those who are totally helpless?"

"We do not have enough men to defeat them, but we may be able to thwart their attempts to move forward with their plans." Ardal put his arm around Fiona's waist.

"I would like to help with that." Grace clasped her hands on the table. "I've spent my whole life defending the law. I can't turn my back on that, but I can use my training to help stop an international organization that is working outside of the law."

Darrogh came into the room at that point. "We will all fight for that. I remember the last battle I fought against the Albireons. They will not give up a planet easily."

"You can also guarantee that if the Albireons have found Earth, then others are here also." Catal spoke in a quiet voice. "They will take an interest in what happens."

"Most are peaceful." Partlan glanced at Grace. "I do not want to see a war on this planet."

"No one does." Ardal cleared his throat. "I think we need to continue helping out the people as we have done in the past. Those that need help can count on us. At the same time, we have to be aware that there is another force at work here."

"Will you be able to assist with that?" Partlan turned to Grace. "The work we do is valuable."

Grace pursed her lips. "I wouldn't be comfortable helping people who have broken the law."

"We bring justice." Ardal explained. "Is that not what the spirit of the law is about?"

Grace nodded. "You're right. I can't deny that sometimes the law doesn't work on behalf of the victims."

"That is where we come in." Ardal tightened his grip on Fiona. "My wife was terrorized by a man who wouldn't quit until he killed her. He had already murdered many women and the law did not stop him. We did."

Grace's eyes widened. "A lot of horrible people fall between the cracks. What about those who are able to change their lives?"

"Niail's mate and children were targeted by a drug lord who controlled the local law enforcement and FBI." Partlan's voice was low. "Even when he was surrounded and given a chance to surrender, the man chose to try and shoot one of us. This is not the type of person who can be rehabilitated."

Catal cleared his throat. "People who want and abuse power will never change."

"Those are the people that have broken our Sacred Code." Ardal's eyes burned with purpose. "They have no honor and are cowards. Our law does not give them a second chance."

"You kill them." Grace's voice was a low whisper. "I find it hard to take a life."

"We all do." Partlan reached over and clasped Grace's hands. "As Hunters, we could not live with ourselves if we let others suffer. That is a greater sin."

Fiona cleared her throat. "I trained to be a doctor. I'm sworn to protect life. I help where I can, but I've learned that I don't always make the right decisions."

"You were not raised to command." Ardal's voice was tender. "On Cygnus, the women make the decisions. We are trained to obey their orders."

Grace nodded. "Only those who have broken your code are killed."

"Yes." Partlan squeezed her hands. "Otherwise, we would be without honor ourselves and unworthy to be Hunters."

Grace frowned. "If that is what you truly do, then I would be willing to help also. I'm trained to fight and I also understand law enforcement procedures."

The tension eased in Partlan's chest. He had not been certain that Grace would be able to find a role by his side. She was used to working to protect the law. Joining with him meant that she would be faced with decisions that went against everything she held sacred. She had agreed to be his mate, but if she could not live with their work as

Hunters, then she would not stay. She needed to be useful, and he understood that on the level that only a pair bond could. She would not help if she thought their work was wrong.

Grace was a warrior.

She understood honor.

"We appreciate your support." Ardal sighed and released Fiona. "Now, we need to consider what to do about Eogan. He is a Hunter and must be our concern."

"He should be rescued." Darrogh's voice was harsh. "It is not right that he be held captive."

"I will try and contact him." Ardal's eyes followed Fiona as she went back to the stove. "He will not ignore our connection."

"He is not always able to connect." Partlan leaned back in his chair. "He will only be able to mind connect when he is away from the facility. I could not reach you when I was there."

"True." Ardal looked over at Lorcan. "Lorcan is mobilizing some of the Hunters in Europe to move into Australia and investigate."

"Surveillance will be tricky." Darrogh crossed his arms over his chest. "We do not want them aware of our existence on this planet."

"They already know we're here." Catal's voice shook. "They are barbaric and I have no problem shutting them down."

"What they did to you, and others that they captured, will be avenged." Ardal's tone was severe. "The Albireons have no honor and have broken many of our codes."

"Eogan must be rescued first." Darrogh's jaw clenched. "We need to protect our own before we destroy the Albireons."

Ardal put his hand on the table. "It is decided. I will contact Eogan and when he is ready, we will rescue him. Until that time, we will continue our work on this planet."

Fiona and Firbin brought plates of food to the table and then sat. Selena was already seated beside Catal. Partlan looked over at Grace and noticed her bow her head for a brief time before she started to eat. She was a woman of many facets. He was privileged to have found such a wonderful and beautiful mate.

He would spend the rest of his life showing her that men of honor could be trusted and relied upon. Never would she have a reason to doubt his commitment or their bond. He would prove to her that destiny had brought them together forever.

Author's Note

The Pine Gap facility was built in 1967 and is a joint venture between the United States and Australia. It is in the center of the Australian continent. Its position makes it impossible for foreign ships to anchor in international waters and do surveillance on the compound. It is cloaked in secrecy and that leads to much speculation about its purpose. Officially, it is a ground satellite station with several large radomes that cover antennae array.

Pine Gap has become Australia's Area 51. Little is known about the actual operations of the facility and this leads to much speculation and rumor. This includes underground tunnels that go to the ocean, below surface cities, and possible connection with extraterrestrials. Strange lights are frequently seen around the base and are thought to be UFOs or advanced technology that is being tested.

About the Author

Cynthia Clement is an award winning author who spent most of her childhood with her nose in a book. She began writing stories in her teens, but it wasn't until her forties that she took her writing seriously.

She enjoys ghost hunting, the paranormal, reading and collecting books, quilting, gardening, and great conversation. She has a BSc in Biology, and a BA in Anthropology and recently graduated from nursing.

Cynthia believes in second chances, exploring new ideas, and bringing the impossible to life. Her novels, whether contemporary, historical, or science fiction, all focus on love, honor, and intrigue.

She lives in Northern Ontario with her husband of thirty-two years, her teenage son, and two dachshunds.

Website: www.cynthiaclement.com

Books by Cynthia Clement

Science Fiction

aHunter4Hire series
aHunter4Rescue
aHunter4Saken
aHunter4Life
aHunter4Ever
aHunter4Trust

Historical

Caldern Family
The Seduction of Sarah
The Seduction of Madalyn

Novellas
Pleasuring Emily
Christmas Kisses